Agent Svetlana Simonov of the top secret Omega Force is on a new and deadly assignment for her government. Two high-ranking American politicians — one a Senator, and the other a Congressmen — hold Top Secret clearances and are leaders in the most critical committees. They've got to be stopped, because every day that goes by, they're selling the country's most sensitive and guarded secrets to enemy governments. Once again, Svetlana is assigned to work with her protégé, the young and lovely Tatiana. Together they face danger and desire on every twist and turn of their assignment.

Double Trouble
Copyright © 2020 Robin Gideon
ISBN: 978-1-4874-3061-0
Cover art by Martine Jardin

Published by eXtasy Books Inc or
Devine Destinies, an imprint of eXtasy Books Inc

Look for us online at:
www.eXtasybooks.com or www.devinedestinies.com

DOUBLE TROUBLE
AGENT (ROM)ANTICS BOOK 4

BY

ROBIN GIDEON

DEDICATION

This one's for Keith. And for Martine, who is damn good.

CHAPTER ONE

Washington D.C.

Svetlana Simonov, agent for Omega Force now for ten years, hadn't expected to get called in by the man who assigned her the missions she went on. But then most of the things that happened to her during the last ten years were things that she hadn't anticipated.

A meeting in a hotel's saloon? In the middle of the afternoon?

In the past, whenever she and he got together, it was always in a private hotel room at some luxury establishment in one of the more fashionable cities of the world. A place where they could be alone so that her controller, a man who called himself Jefferson Burke, though Svetlana knew that only the "Burke" part was actually his real name, could speak to her privately. He could question her about her last mission, and give her instructions regarding her next mission.

But there was always something more than just what he had to tell her, and for that *something more* they needed privacy, and generally, several hours of uninterrupted together-time. That was when Burke would dispense his considerable sensual skills, which invariably would cause four or more climaxes to explode through Svetlana's senses with the effect of a hand grenade going off inside an aluminum mailbox.

This time there's got to be something truly, desperately wrong. Otherwise he wouldn't have changed our routine.

A shiver went through her as she walked down the

1

sidewalk, her stiletto heels clicking against the concrete, her eyes open but hardly seeing either the sidewalk or the people around her. All thoughts were on Burke and his mysterious and unexpected request that she meet him in the Montgomery Hotel saloon promptly at three o'clock.

Omega Force is being disbanded. That's got to be it. What will I do without Omega Force?

She'd been with the mysterious organization since she was eighteen, when they plucked her out of boot camp and turned her into an assassin. She couldn't imagine a life when she *wasn't* in Omega Force.

It was in Omega Force that Burke had taught her how to kill and taught her how to make love.

He'd taught her everything she had needed to know about doing those two things. When she considered it now, he'd taught her everything she knew that was of any importance.

And then he'd taught her more. He taught her that, in her heart of hearts, she was a submissive and, like a true soul-mate, he was her Dominant. She had learned from him that with her hands tied behind her back with his silk necktie, she could feel simultaneously powerless and yet like the most emancipated woman in the world. There was something particularly powerful about the climaxes he gave her when she was in bondage.

As she walked, something caught her attention, freeing her from her reverie, which she welcomed. Svetlana stopped walking abruptly and looked up, blinking her eyes several times to orient herself once again to her physical surroundings.

The hotel, which was the source of her destination, was just twenty yards ahead of her, and to her right. Svetlana told herself that she shouldn't let her mind wander so, that to allow such intellectual meanderings was to put herself in jeopardy. It was foolish to not be aware of her surroundings. She had enemies who might at that moment be plotting to put a bullet to the back of her head, delivered without a word of warning.

Svetlana shrugged this off.

She wasn't in danger, because the only man in the world who knew what she really did was waiting for her in the hotel's saloon, and if he wanted to kill her, there wasn't anything she could do to stop him. He knew too much about her, and she knew almost nothing about him.

As she approached the saloon's front door, she checked her appearance in the window. She had chosen to wear a casual blue dress that belted at the waist and showed only a modest amount of cleavage or thigh. There were times when being sartorially daring was appropriate, but she didn't think this was one of them.

She wasn't wearing a garter belt or stockings, and she second guessed herself now because she hadn't. Burke always liked seeing her in nice lingerie, she knew. He had told her as much, and she liked to please him whenever possible.

At least I put on pretty pink panties and bra. He'll like seeing me in those.

It was some consolation, but not a lot. Svetlana promised herself that the next time she got a call from Burke to meet, she'd be wearing the full ensemble of matching garter belt, silk stockings, bikini panties, and brassiere. All the lovely, feminine lingerie that Burke liked to see her in—right before he ripped most of them off her body, then ravished her like a truly Dominant madman until she had climaxed three or four times. Sometimes, when Burke was at his absolute Dom best and they hadn't been together in quite a while, she climaxed six or seven times during their feverish rather sweaty hours-long encounter.

Remembering those times made Svetlana shiver. She pushed those thoughts away. This wasn't the time for reminiscing.

She looked at her wristwatch, the gold one with sparkling diamonds to indicate the hours. It was one minute to three o'clock. Burke always insisted that she be extraordinarily punctual, practically down to the second. If ever she wasn't, he would generally punish her by putting her over his knee, pulling her dress up and her panties down, and delivering a severe spanking that turned the pale cheeks of her bottom bring pink, and sometimes very close to red. And that was only the beginning of the punishment. There was always so much more than that.

With fifteen seconds to go, Svetlana opened the front door to the hotel's saloon and stepped inside. She stopped immediately, because it had been quite sunny outside, and the saloon itself was quite dark. For several seconds she was sightless, unable to see anything at all except a neon sign behind the long mahogany bar, advertising a beer she had never heard of.

"Over here."

The deep, masculine voice was familiar to her, and immediately whatever misgivings or insecurities Svetlana had previously experienced disappeared like a puff of smoke in gale force winds. The man she knew as Jefferson Burke represented to her nothing less than absolute security. She trusted him with not just her life and her heart, but with her soul.

Svetlana had to wait several seconds until her vision adjusted enough before she started walking toward the comforting voice she had heard. She hadn't taken three steps before she stopped with the abruptness of a woman who had been stuck in the forehead with the heel of a palm—hard.

She saw Burke sitting in a booth, handsome as ever in a hand-tailored suit of navy blue. But on the other side of the booth was a young blonde girl that Svetlana knew perhaps more intimately that she was comfortable admitting. Her name was—at least it was *now*, after she had been recruited into Omega Force straight out of boot camp—Tatiana Simonov. And her cover, as created by Omega Force, was that she was Svetlana's younger sister, by a decade.

They had worked together for Omega Force before, and the things that they had done to each other while on that mission were things that sisters never did to each other. Never. But she and Tatiana had.

"Tatiana," Svetlana said softly, standing now at the edge of the booth. She could feel her heart begin to race. The prospect of seeing Burke had, of course, elevated her heart rate. But seeing Tatiana in the booth with him had added an emotional elements to this encounter that Svetlana had not anticipated.

Tatiana looked into her eyes and said softly, "Svetlana." Several seconds passed before she added, "It's good to see you again."

Svetlana wondered whether the teenager was lying. They shared a history. Svetlana hadn't thought she'd ever see Tatiana again.

Burke, as handsome as ever, rose from the booth, bent down, and kissed Svetlana on the cheek. It was a chaste kiss. Suddenly, shooting across the surface of her mind while Burke's warm and far too kissable lips were still on her cheek, she remembered *exactly* what it felt like when Burke's kisses weren't chaste.

And when they sure as hell weren't on her cheek. There wasn't a part of her body that he hadn't tasted and tantalized.

Burke said, "Please sit."

Svetlana had a decision to make. She could either sit on Burke's side of the booth, or on Tatiana's.

It was impossible for her to rationally make a decision between the two. Both had given her climaxes that she'd never forget.

In a soft voice, Tatiana said, "Please, sit next to me" as she slid slightly across the bench seat of the booth. She appeared, at that moment, quite young and innocent. Svetlana was aware of this, and felt both aroused and guilty for her feelings.

Svetlana sat. Looking directly at Burke, Svetlana said, "I had thought we'd be alone."

There was accusation of wrongdoing, or at least deception, in her tone.

"I'm sorry," Burke said, his lips temporarily compressed. "Something has come up that's requiring immediate attention. We've got to act on it instantly because every second counts." He looked at Svetlana, then at Tatiana. "This is a bad one. One of the worst security breaches I've ever seen."

Svetlana felt a chill go through her. Burke wasn't the kind of man who exaggerated the danger of a situation. Not when it came to national security.

A waitress stepped forward, though she remained about ten feet from the booth. Svetlana realized that Burke had given her forewarning that privacy was to be maintained.

"We'd like a round," Burke said.

Svetlana watched him smile, and immediately saw the waitress's favorable response to it. For several seconds she had to try very hard to not resent the young woman for responding romantically to Burke's gorgeous smile.

"For myself," Burke said, "I'd like an Irish whiskey, on the rocks. And I won't assume to have the authority to speak for you ladies." It was a generous statement. She knew that Burke often made decisions for others. Very often, whether it was wanted or not.

Svetlana said, making a peevish point of doing it before Tatiana, "I'll have a vodka martini, three-to-one vodka to vermouth, and garnished with three stuffed olives."

She and Tatiana exchanged a look. There was no rancor in it, and Svetlana felt rather guilty for her own unattractive behavior, even if she had pretty much kept the emotion to herself. She promised herself she'd make amends soon.

"I'll have the same," Tatiana said. She smiled at Svetlana. "It sounds delicious."

The waitress looked at Tatiana, then at Burke and, after several seconds of silence, said, "But . . ."

Burke shot the bar manager a cold-eyed look. The manager reacted immediately.

"Make sure their drinks are all on the house," he told the waitress.

"That won't be necessary. I'll be buying," Burke said.

In a soft voice, the waitress said, "I'm sorry. My mistake. Please forgive me."

"Nothing to forgive." Burke's tone was the very essence of kindness. "You've been nothing less than delightful."

There are about fifty good reasons to love that man, and he's just shown one of them.

Flittering across the surface of her mind came a myriad of possibilities on just exactly how she might prove to him that she loved him, but Svetlana tried to push them more toward the back of her consciousness. When she was with Burke, thoughts of being on her knees or on her back were always only just seconds away.

But there was also Tatiana to think about, since she was sitting close enough to her left that Svetlana could feel her thigh against her own. Then Svetlana remembered that in the past, she had felt more than just Tatiana's thigh touching her.

Stop thinking that way.

Silence descended upon the trio until the drinks came, and after the waitress served then exited, Burke lifted his drink and said, "To a successful and safe mission."

They clinked glasses. Svetlana took a sip of her drink, then a second. She wanted a certain level of fortification, since she wasn't at all confident about what was going on now or what would happen in the future.

After making certain that they were in a place in the saloon where no one could hear them, Burke cleared his throat, then leaned toward the table, closer to the women. Svetlana understood the body posture. What he was about to say was important to national security, and Svetlana needed to pay careful attention to every word.

"We've got a situation where some politicians in high places are selling our government's secrets to a country that most definitely is an enemy. The politicians are guilty as hell, but we can't say anything about it because if we do, then we let our enemies know how we got the information, and the first thing they'll do is change all their operational plans. If that happens, we'll be at Ground Zero, like we were from the very beginning."

"So, we've got to stop them, but do it in such a manner that the bad guys won't know how it is that we know what they know?" Svetlana asked. She felt her palms get clammy. This was a new kind of mission for her.

"This means that it can't be an executive action," Burke said, then made a disdainful face briefly.

Executive action? Ha. Such a nice euphemism for assassination.

There were times when she wished — most times, actually — that the people she worked for and the government she worked for would simply come right out and say what they actually meant. Executive action? When an executive in a Fortune 500 company made a decision, that was an executive action. When someone at Omega Force decided that an enemy of the state must be killed, that was an assassination.

She loathed the fact that some people were making a CEO executive's decision the same as a death sentence.

Well, at least for once they're not asking me to kill anyone.

Svetlana began to think that this mission might not be so bad after all . . . even if she did have a partner.

"These men have got to be destroyed politically, and as quickly as possible," Burke said, then took a sip of his drink.

Svetlana watched as the muscles in his shoulders tightened, then relaxed. He was becoming comfortable in discussing the assignment, she realized, and she wondered whether he would invite her up to his hotel room later. It was something she always looked forward to with unalloyed anticipation. Beneath the table, she crossed her legs at the knee, and felt a soft but gentle tingling begin in her clitoris. This meeting was getting better by the second.

"They're selling our most sensitive secrets regarding surface-to-air defenses, where and how our submarines are being deployed, and how we're keeping them hidden."

Tatiana said, "But those are two entirely different segments of our military."

Svetlana was surprised but pleased that Tatiana had immediately realized that.

"The politicians are on two separate committees, one in the House of Representatives, the other in the Senate. They were both approached by the same government." Burke closed his eyes for the briefest moment. "We're bleeding top secret information, and every day that goes by, we bleed a little more." He groaned as though in physical pain. "They're in the highest level, most senior positions on two critical committees. They've got access to everything, and they're selling everything they get their hands on."

Svetlana said, "So we've got to take them down without killing them, and whatever we do it's got to seem as though we didn't know they were bent. If we do, the bad guys will reverse engineer what we've done, and shut the system down. If that happens, we'll have won the battle but lost the war."

"Exactly," Burke said. "Since there's two of them, and this takedown has to happen as quickly as possible, you're both assigned." He closed his eyes once again, took a sip of his cocktail, then looked directly into Tatiana's eyes. "However, inquiries have been made recently. We've put together a pretty good background cover for you, but there are certain bad actors in the world who are questioning it. Before I'm comfortable sending you out on another assignment, we've got to figure out some way of making the false background Omega Force has written for you seem so legitimate that only a paranoid fool would question it."

Svetlana asked, "How's my cover?"

She felt marrow-deep relief when Burke look at her and replied, "As solid as granite. After all these years, it's not doubted. It's not even questioned."

It hasn't been all that *many years.*

She wanted to tell him that, but didn't. It *had* been years of operating undercover, and that meant she'd been under constant, unending psychological pressure. She couldn't pretend otherwise.

Without entirely thinking through what she was about to say, Svetlana looked at Burke, placed her hand on the warm, velvety thigh of Tatiana, midway between her knee and hip, and said, "I know just how we're going to solidify Tatiana's cover story so that it's never questioned again."

CHAPTER TWO

Tatiana was simultaneously aware of the fact that she was both intimidated by Svetlana from the top of her head down to the tips of her toes, and impressed with her more thoroughly and completely than she ever had been with any woman in her life. She understood that these emotions were often at war within her.

"When we're finished with this little game," Svetlana said as she pulled the cork from the opened bottle she had ordered from room service, "there won't be any question at all in anyone's mind that you're my kid sister, and that you're everything that Omega Force's fake dossier says you are."

Standing in Burke's hotel room, Tatiana watched as Svetlana poured two glasses of sparkling champagne, set the bottle back in the ice bucket, then poured from a one-serving plastic bottle of Irish whiskey that had been extracted from the room's mini-refrigerator, into a lowball glass filled with ice.

She handed Tatiana a glass. When Tatiana took the glass, she was a little surprised that her own hand wasn't shaking even slightly. She didn't know what was going to happen, but she was confident that with Svetlana making the decisions, she had no reason to fear.

"Get your phone out," Svetlana said to Burke. She clinked her glass to Tatiana's. "I get this feeling this is going to be a bumpy ride, but in the end, we'll accomplish everything we've set out to do."

Tatiana took a sip of her champagne. It was icy cold,

sinfully delicious . . . and Tatiana suspected that this wouldn't be the last glass she'd be drinking this afternoon.

She still had only suspicions about what Svetlana had in mind, but she could feel a small but insistent throbbing in her pussy, and though she couldn't say precisely why, she suspected that somehow Svetlana was responsible for that erotic pulsation, and that there would come a time when she would be eternally grateful for it.

Svetlana took another sip of champagne. When she looked into Burke's eyes, Tatiana could tell that he didn't have any more of an idea of what Svetlana had planned that she did — but like her, he trusted Svetlana completely.

"You mustn't speak," Svetlana said to Burke, "because they'll figure out who you are through voice recognition." She smiled coquettishly. "And, of course, your face must never be on video . . . even if other parts of you are."

Tatiana watched as Svetlana tipped her champagne glass back, swallowing its contents, then refilled it. Tatiana was only slightly surprised when Svetlana touched the underside of her glass, indicating Tatiana was to drink. She kept her fingers to the bottom of the glass until Tatiana had finished it entirely. Then she filled it up.

Svetlana turned to Burke and said, "Better start the video. We're going to need enough minutes so that Tatiana's cover story is as solid as mine."

Oh, God, now I know what she's got in mind.

As Burke held up his cell phone and started the video, Svetlana looked at him, smiling as she raised her champagne glass, and in an exaggerated, slightly slurred manner, in Russian-accented English, said, "I've always believed that a close family is a happy family."

Then, to Tatiana but in Russian, she said, "And you believe that, don't you?"

Tatiana inhaled deeply, and the breath caught in her throat. She looked at Svetlana, then at the camera recording her every movement.

What the hell am I supposed to do?

Tatiana brought her champagne glass to her lips, tilted her head back, and swallowing several times. She didn't stop until she had drained the glass.

"Sisters," Tatiana said in Russian. Then "sisters" in thickly accented English.

She watched as Svetlana closed the distance that separated them, and was erotically aware of the taut movement of Svetlana's breasts as she walked, and of the delicate scent of Chanel No. 5 that drifted from her like a heavenly aura.

Turning toward the camera, Svetlana said, "You love us." She was close enough for Tatiana to feel the heat of her body — or so it seemed. "Both? It would be such a shame if you didn't love us both . . . because we love each other so much, and we love you. You can't love one of us unless you love both of us."

Tatiana suspected she should say something at that moment. She understood that she was playing a role for the camera, but she wasn't at all certain what that particular role was supposed to be.

"Let's show him what he's got coming," Svetlana said in English. And then in Russian she added, loud enough for it to be recorded, "And this is just the beginning."

Svetlana eased her fingers beneath the fall of Tatiana's hair at the back of her neck, and Tatiana would have sworn at that moment that the touch of those fingertips against her skin was the most erotic thing she had ever felt.

She tilted her head back on her shoulders, and Tatiana was quite suddenly aware of the height difference between herself and Svetlana. She was five-foot-one and wearing flat sandals, and Svetlana was five-foot-nine and wearing five-inch stilettos.

Quite suddenly, the full mounds of Svetlana's breasts were disturbingly at face-level.

"God," Tatiana whispered.

"Has nothing to do with this," Svetlana countered without a moment's hesitation, then bent at the waist and slanted her mouth over Tatiana's.

When Svetlana's tongue eased between her lips and delved deeply into her mouth, Tatiana hoped that her bones wouldn't suddenly melt because of the eroticism of the kiss, though she strongly suspected that they might. A kiss from Svetlana had that effect on her.

Her arms remained at her sides as Svetlana kissed her, but her legs had seemed to turn to jelly. It took a conscious act of willpower for Tatiana to keep her knees from buckling beneath her while Svetlana feasted on her mouth with the slow, savoring action of a connoisseur who believed that a woman's lips were the most delicious meal the gods had ever produced.

Then, without warning, Svetlana ended the kiss, and Tatiana found herself gasping for air and rather disoriented, trying to figure out what the hell had just happened.

She blinked her eyes several times, then watched as Svetlana turned toward Burke and his camera.

"As you can see, Tatiana and I are rather closer than most sisters. Actually . . . there's much more to see . . . and you get to be the one to see it."

What does that mean?

Without a moment's hesitation, Svetlana turned back toward Tatiana, and sealed her mouth down over hers. But this time, it wasn't just a kiss on the lips that she was satisfied with. This time, as her tongue entered Tatiana's mouth and began its intimate dance, Svetlana's hand moved from Tatiana's hip up to the small, extraordinarily sensitive mound of Tatiana's right breast.

"Ohhh," Tatiana moaned when she felt confident, feminine fingers closing around her breast. "God."

Firm experienced fingers captured her nipple through her

blouse and bra. Sizzling pleasure shot through her veins at the caress, but a soft squeal of protest still came from her throat.

She was intensely aroused, but there was also the awareness that Burke was right there, and even more importantly, he was taking video of what Svetlana was doing to her. Tatiana shivered, but she did nothing to push Svetlana's hand from her breast, or to end the kiss that was rapidly turning her blood into something more resembling molten lava.

Svetlana eventually ended the kisses, and with her lips still touching Tatiana's, she whispered, "I know we're just supposed to pretend — as Omega Force agents — that this is just a game for the camera, but the truth is I'd kiss you anywhere, anytime, with anyone watching, under any conditions."

"Really?" The single word came out of Tatiana's mouth as something of a gasp. She felt her nipples harden perceptibly.

"Even if there wasn't a camera," Svetlana whispered, now directly into Tatiana's ear, "I'd want to give you pleasure." She kissed Svetlana's neck. "I'd want to eat your pussy."

"Oh, God," Tatiana gasped when the full impact of Svetlana's last comment fully registered in her brain. And then, seconds later when she felt Svetlana's teeth nipping tantalizingly on her throat, she said aloud, "Svetlana." She said the single name in a manner that was almost a prayer, something that was nearly sexual idolatry.

Svetlana removed Tatiana's clothes as they sat on the edge of the hotel's king-sized bed. The clothes were removed slowly, because that was the way that Svetlana wanted to do it, and Tatiana was in no mood to argue.

First the blouse came off, the buttons unfastened with gentle deliberation while Burke took video of each sensual action. Then Tatiana's bra was unfastened and removed, and Tatiana's breasts were revealed to Svetlana, Burke, and the camera.

"You have the most beautiful breasts in the world,"

Svetlana said in a breathy whisper.

Tatiana didn't know if she was saying those flattering words because she was on camera, or if she was telling the truth.

She desperately hoped that Svetlana was speaking honestly. Especially when, a moment later, she felt Svetlana's lips surround her right nipple, and the warmth and moisture of her mouth suffused every aroused nerve in Tatiana's body.

Tatiana was aware of Burke moving about, but she was unwilling to open her eyes when such pleasure was going through her, and if she was being truthful with herself, she really wasn't interested in knowing what he was doing. What was arousing was that a very beautiful woman was sucking on her nipple, and a very handsome man was not only watching her as this happened, he was also taking video of it. Burke's presence added *sooo* much to the eroticism of the moment.

She felt Svetlana release her nipple from between her lips, then begin to kiss down her stomach. As she did, she began removing Tatiana's skirt, and did so with more urgency than artfulness. When the zipper to Tatiana's skirt refused to cooperate, Svetlana simply pulled the skirt wider apart, with the accompanying sound of very expensive fabric being torn by brute force, then jerked the garment over the curve of her hips.

She's not a woman who allows her wishes to be thwarted.

The thought made Tatiana shiver, because it said a thousand things about Svetlana's passion that she really had not known before, and put another very fine point on her own acceptance of being dominated by another woman — specifically, Svetlana.

Oh, yes. This is a day with real potential.

In Russian, Svetlana said, clearly for the camera, "You've made me wait all night to taste your pussy. If I was any sister at all, I'd tell you to go to hell and walk away from this sweet body of yours."

Tatiana's mind was spinning. She knew that Svetlana was playing a game for the camera, but she didn't know exactly what her own role was supposed to be. Was she to be bold, or shy? Demanding, or subservient? All she was certain of was that Burke and Svetlana understood this game a thousand times better than she did. She would trust them.

Svetlana didn't rip off her panties, though she did jerk them over the curve of Tatiana's hips and down her legs in a move that both bordered on violence, and brought Tatiana precipitously close to climaxing.

"God," Tatiana said. It seemed the right thing to say.

"Is not with us right now," Svetlana said, finishing the sentence. Then, with a hand to Tatiana's shoulder, Svetlana shoved her forcibly backward with enough strength that she bounced on the mattress.

Svetlana grabbed Tatiana's ankles and spread them obscenely wide apart. Tatiana thought then that her heart was pounding so hard it must surely be heard by Svetlana and Burke. When she looked at Burke, she saw that he was holding the camera steadily, recording every lurid detail of what was being done to her. She also noted that his trousers were now struggling to contain a massive erection that was furious about being imprisoned within clothing not designed for well-endowed men who had something rather more interested on their mind than what was happening on Wall Street.

Tatiana was looking at Burke's bulging trousers, thinking that she would not mind it at all if he told her it was her duty as a field agent of Omega Force to suck his cock, when she felt Svetlana's mouth press erotically against the lips of her cunt.

"Ahhh," Tatiana exclaimed, her eyes rolling back in her head as she felt a warm, feminine tongue separate the lips of her pussy.

The fact that the lips and tongue currently tantalizing her

cunt were experienced in such matters was glaringly, blissfully apparent. From the very beginning, Tatiana was aware that she wasn't the first woman that Svetlana had pleasured. It thrilled her, though, to at least be *one* of the *many*. She was almost grateful, and would have been had raw lust not muddied her thinking.

She almost said "God" once again, but managed to silence herself before that word passed between her lips. It was difficult, though, to not call out to deities when so many thoroughly heavenly feelings were bombarding her senses.

Tatiana placed a forearm over her closed eyes. A semblance of modesty made her want to hide herself from the video camera which was recording behavior that Tatiana could not have even imagined herself doing months earlier.

Once she had become an agent for Omega Force, *everything* in her life had changed. Everything.

And some of it much for the better.

The thought caused her to smile, even as she lay on her back with her knees raised and spread wide apart while an utterly gorgeous woman was sucking lightly and lovingly on her clitoris.

This isn't really happening to me. It can't be.

She moved her forearm away from her eyes, then turned her head to look at Burke. He was standing at the edge of the bed, holding the all-seeing camera steady. Knowing that there would be video of what she was doing added fuel to the inferno going on inside Tatiana. She hadn't thought of herself as an exhibitionist, but now she knew a secret about herself she'd previously been unaware of.

Softly, as though she wasn't very confident of what she was saying, Tatiana said almost conversationally, "I'm going to come."

Twenty seconds later, when everything in her body suddenly tightened so severely it was at that moment sheer agony, Tatiana began screaming, the sound of her voice bouncing off the walls of the hotel room as wave after wave of ecstasy flowed over her.

It was some minutes later, after the last of the wrenching contractions had gone through her, that Tatiana opened her eyes and looked down the front of her perspiring body and between her thighs at the beautiful face of the woman who had just provided the splendid series of climaxes that had satisfied every sensual impulse in her body.

"You can stop now," Tatiana said, her breathing deep and uneven. Under the circumstances, that didn't surprise her. "Lovely." She sighed. "Is it okay to say that what you just did to me was lovely? I hope so, because I can't think of any other word to describe what you just made me feel."

"Tatiana, if you think this is over," Svetlana said in Russian, "you're the most naïve little sister on the planet."

Tatiana was surprised, but not in the least bit dismayed, when Svetlana stretched out over her, her clothed body warm and voluptuous against Tatiana's naked one. Svetlana placed her palms lightly along the sides of Tatiana's face, their noses nearly touching.

"Kiss me now, and you'll taste your own passion on my lips."

It was a bold, erotic statement, and Tatiana felt her sex clench. Then, very slowly, Svetlana dipped her head down. When Tatiana inhaled, she could, in fact, catch the evocative scent of her own pussy on Svetlana's lips. The scent aroused her.

"Kiss me," Tatiana heard herself say. She spoke in English, for the benefit of the camera. "I want to taste my cunt on your lips." She looked straight into Svetlana's eyes. "And after I taste myself on your lips . . . then I want to taste your cunt."

They kissed, and when they did, Tatiana trembled as passion blossomed anew in her soul. She wrapped her legs around Svetlana's hips, locking her heels together as though she would never release Svetlana from her lustful embrace.

For several seconds Tatiana tried to tell herself that she was merely acting, doing what was necessary for the camera's benefit, for the false dossier that Omega Force had invented. But she knew in her heart that this wasn't true. As she swirled her tongue with Svetlana's, there wasn't a single, sensual nerve in her body that wasn't vibrantly aroused. Her naked nipples, pressed against Svetlana's more voluptuous, clothed breasts, were so fiercely erect they throbbed with a tension that was almost painful.

It was Svetlana who ended the kiss, and though Tatiana wanted to complain, she did not. An hour's worth of non-stop kissing wouldn't have been enough to satisfy Tatiana's passionate hunger for them.

Svetlana moved slowly but deliberately, first pushing Tatiana's naked legs apart, then crawling slowly upward on the bed, easing her clothed body along Tatiana's naked one, sliding against her inch by inch, evocatively moving upward.

Svetlana had to spread her knees wide apart to straddle Tatiana's head.

Tatiana looked up into Svetlana's crystal blue eyes as she pulled her panties aside to reveal the most beautiful vagina in the world.

"You know what to do," Svetlana said, steel determination in the words. "I'll let you know when you can stop."

CHAPTER THREE

Svetlana tried to remember how many times she had climaxed, realized she didn't really know, and told herself that having had too many climaxes to remember was a good thing. A *very* good thing.

She thought about getting a pillow to put under her knees, then decided against it. This certainly wasn't the first time she'd been in front of Burke with her knees on the carpeted floor of a hotel room, and it undoubtedly wouldn't be the last. Besides, the carpet was quite plush, and the cock that was pointed straight at her face was quite large. Very large, actually. And beautiful. Svetlana suspected that she shouldn't think of Burke's cock as beautiful, but the fact of the matter was, it *was* beautiful.

Facts are facts.

Svetlana finished her glass of icy cold champagne, set it on the floor near her hip, then looked over at Tatiana, who was sitting on the hotel's king-sized bed, also sipping a glass of champagne that had been chilled to the perfect temperature of forty-seven degrees.

"Let me feast for a little while," Svetlana said, her lips nuzzling the head of Burke's cock as she spoke, "but then you can join. I'm willing to share him with you, but not just yet." Rather theatrically, she licked the length of Burke's cock from the base to the head, then used the tip of her tongue against the slit of his crown.

Burke groaned from the pleasure that Svetlana elicited, and she felt her pussy get just a little bit wetter, a fraction more sensitive.

I love my life.

Svetlana hadn't had that thought in quite a long time, but as she did now, she filled her mouth with Burke's cock, taking the plump crown between her lips. She tightened her lips around the shaft before putting her tongue to work on the sensitive underside, which she knew from experience Burke greatly appreciated.

"God."

Svetlana heard the word, and though she kept Burke's cock buried deep in her mouth, she looked to her right. Tatiana was now sitting on the edge of the bed with her knees spread wide. Her right hand was at the juncture of her thighs, and it was moving slowly back and forth.

The fact that Tatiana was finger-fucking herself while watching a blow job being given heightened Svetlana's arousal.

She tilted her head back on her shoulders and looked up at Burke, who was still taking lurid video.

He's gorgeous.

Svetlana took Burke's cock out of her mouth, kissed it twice just to let him know exactly what she thought of him, and asked, "Do you want her to suck your cock? I'm sure she's dying to." After a couple seconds, she added, "But I'm better at it than she is."

Fuck. I'm more insecure than I thought.

She turned to Tatiana and said, "I won't be selfish. Would you like some of this?"

"I would."

It infuriated Svetlana from the top of her head down to the tips of her toes that Tatiana all but leaped at the opportunity to have Burke's cock in her mouth.

"Me, too," Tatiana enthused, settling on her knees beside Svetlana. The look on her face suggested that she had just been told that there really was a Santa Claus, and that he was standing right in front of her, and if she was a *really* bad girl, she was about to have a *really* good night.

Svetlana was trying very hard to not resent Tatiana with every drop of blood that flowed through her veins.

"That's big," Tatiana said. She looked over at Svetlana. She caught her lower lip between her teeth for a moment in an impish, innocent way. "That's very big."

Stating the obvious makes me less inclined to share him with you.

Making little effort to keep petty jealousy out of her tone, Svetlana said, "I'm pretty sure that he'd prefer it if you'd suck more and talk less."

Even Svetlana realized that it was a particularly catty thing to say, but she was feeling edgy and insecure, and she didn't like the feelings at all.

With her fingers surrounding the base of Burke's cock, Svetlana angled the hard flesh so that the crown was pointed toward Tatiana.

"Go ahead," she said softly, hardly able to comprehend the fact that she was about to share Burke's cock with another woman. Then, with more honesty than she'd planned, she said, "If I have to share him, better with you than with anyone else."

When she watched Tatiana begin licking the head of Burke's cock, Svetlana felt only a little remorse. When Tatiana opened her lips and took the succulent flesh into her mouth, a surge of resentment went through Svetlana, but she tamped the emotion down swiftly, knowing that nothing good could come of it.

"You're so beautiful," Svetlana whispered as Tatiana began swanning her head and shoulders. Svetlana hadn't intended on being that honest.

Svetlana held Burke in her right hand, but with her left she stroked Tatiana's silky blonde hair. She had never seen anything that was quite so erotic when, from only inches away, Tatiana took the lust-swollen head of Burke's cock in and out of her mouth. The girl's eyes were closed. She seemed very nearly in a trance. Svetlana leaned forward and lightly kissed Tatiana's temple as the last vestiges of jealousy and resentment were released from her soul.

She licked the circumference of Tatiana's ear, then whispered, "Isn't he delicious?"

Tatiana replied, "Um-hum," without ever stopping her undulations.

Svetlana dipped her head down and briefly sucked on Tatiana's pink left nipple. When the girl moaned, Svetlana reached between her slender thighs to press the flat of her fingers against sex lips that were dewy with desire.

She loves his cock as much as I do.

Svetlana eased her middle finger between the lips of Tatiana's pussy, and when she did, she felt fresh cream come to the lips of her own pussy. A shiver went through her.

"I should be jealous of you, but I'm not," Svetlana said, sliding her finger in and out of Tatiana as she sucked slowly on Burke's cock, savoring what he had for her like a gourmet leisurely consuming a sumptuous meal cooked by a master chef. "You're the only woman in the world I'm willing to share him with."

She bent low, then, and once again began sucking on Tatiana's nipples while Tatiana sucked on Burke's cock. The low, soft moans that Tatiana emitted let Svetlana know that everything that was being done aroused her. Svetlana's finger slid smoothly in and out of Tatiana's cunt, and with each invasion and retreat, fresh cream lubricated the tight channel.

"Tell me what you want," Svetlana whispered. "Do you want to swallow his cum, or do you want to feel his cock inside you?"

Tatiana leaned back far enough to get Burke's cock out of her mouth. She looked at Svetlana and said in a whisper so soft it was hardly audible, "Inside me. Please? You don't mind? I'm not asking for too much?"

Svetlana kissed Tatiana's lips softly, quickly, and asked, "You've never been with him before?"

"Never," Tatiana replied with sincerity.

"Then, my darling Tatiana, you're in for an experience unlike anything you've ever had before."

Svetlana looked up into Burke's face. He was still holding his camera, taking both video and audio of everything that Svetlana and Tatiana were doing to him.

"Would it be asking too much if you would please fuck her?"

I've never felt so full of cock in my life.

This utterly intemperate thought came to Tatiana as, simultaneously, she felt Burke slide the entire length of his cock into her pussy, and Svetlana lower her hips enough to press her cunt against Tatiana's mouth.

The best of both worlds.

Tatiana snaked her arms around Svetlana's naked thighs, and as she did so, she wondered when Svetlana had taken her clothes off. After more orgasms that she could remember, Tatiana had discovered that there were gaps in her memory — in her consciousness — when she was making love with Svetlana and Burke. This didn't particularly disturb her, though she was aware of the fact that it was a new phenomenon for her.

Come for me. Both of you.

Tatiana closed her lips around the pink, erect clit that Svetlana was only too willing to feed her.

She opened her eyes to see Svetlana, her face angled downward though her eyes were closed, breathing through parted lips. Quite obviously, she was enjoying what Tatiana was doing to her, and because she did enjoy it, Tatiana was all the more eager to provide the pleasure.

Without taking her mouth entirely away from Svetlana,

Tatiana said softly, "Come for me." And then, seconds later, she added, "Come for me while he's got his cock inside me." She caressed Svetlana's thighs with her fingertips, and at that moment knew with absolute certainty that there was never skin more velvety than that which her fingers now caressed. "Please, I want you to come on my mouth."

Tatiana got significantly more than she had wished for when she experienced the utter bliss of Svetlana coming on her mouth while she climaxed as Burke thrust his cock into her with furious energy. Tatiana was just descending from an orgasmic stratosphere when she heard Burke growl low in his throat, and she knew that he was releasing his passion deep inside her.

Tatiana had never felt more sexual, more confident, or more satisfied, than she did at that very moment.

She kissed Svetlana's pussy, then in a cheeky manner, asked, "How did I do? And if I wasn't all that you hoped for, be gentle. I can be insecure about these things. I promise, I'll get better as you do this to me more often."

CHAPTER FOUR

Los Angeles, California

I *cannot believe that this is happening to me.*
Amira Marx was standing in a line of seven people waiting to get into the California Club. If there was anything that Amira believed in life, it was that she should never—not *ever*—wait in a line to get into a nightclub or restaurant. Women like her simply didn't have to suffer such indignities. Never. It shouldn't matter than she didn't have a reservation.

She looked at the doorkeeper, a man who was clearly hired because the breath of his shoulders was measured in yards, not inches.

He's got to be new to not recognize me.

Standing just behind Amira were two women that Amira had never seen before. They, like her, looked bored and entirely unamused with the fact that they had to wait in line to get into the club. It was obvious they had wealth.

"There you are," the doorkeeper said suddenly, hurrying forward.

When he walked right past Amira to get to the two blonde women, Amira promised herself that she was going to make the doorman pay for his snub with nothing less than blood.

"We've been waiting for you," the doorman said, his smile honest, every expression he made indicating that there was no one on the planet that he wanted to see more than the two blondes dressed in designer clothes and wearing jewelry that cost more than the GDP of most South American countries.

The doorkeeper ushered the two blondes into the club without a second's hesitation.

From directly behind her, Amira heard her husband, David, say, "I don't know who those two are, but you can guarantee that I sure as fuck am going to find out within the hour."

"If we ever get in this place," Amira said peevishly, though she took a certain pleasure in hearing the annoyance David had at being denied immediate entrance into the club. "Be patient, my love. I'm sure they'll realize the error of their ways in just a matter of seconds."

"They'd better," David said with softly spoken venom. "They goddamned well better."

Seconds later, David and Amira Marx were escorted into the roped-off VIP section of the nightclub. Only the most elite clientele were allowed behind the rope.

As Amira took her seat and a waitress hurried forward, David said, "Who the hell are they?"

"Find out," his wife said, with venom in her voice that was just loud enough to hear over the electronic dance music. "Tonight." She said the single word with finality. "The sooner, the better."

The two women in question were seated at a table next to Amira's. One was in her late twenties, and she had the kind of beauty that women of every country and culture wished they had, but only she possessed. The other was a decade or so younger, and Amira wondered if she was even old enough to be legally drinking alcohol in an American nightclub.

The thought of the young woman being denied alcohol in an establishment that specialized in catering to the most affluent people in Hollywood flittered through her consciousness, but then she immediately dismissed it as foolishness. In the most influential cities of the world, unimaginable wealth bought privileges that common people not only didn't have, they couldn't even understand.

It's just the way it is. And I like it that way.

Amira understood this, even if very few people around her did.

Their drinks arrived, and Amira leaned toward David and asked, "Do you think they're beautiful?" When her husband nodded, she asked, "Which one would you like to fuck first?"

David looked directly into her eyes and said, "The one you want to watch me fucking first."

Amira smiled. "Right answer."

"They're looking at us," Svetlana said, keeping her voice low, just loud enough for Tatiana to hear above the piped-in dance music. "So far, so good."

She looked over at Tatiana and wondered how many fears were ricocheting through her mind. She was new to this game of espionage, and she most certainly hadn't time to prepare herself emotionally for this assignment. In fact, hardly had Burke explained what they needed to do before she and Tatiana were on a plane headed for California.

Svetlana had enough experience to accept the fact that sometimes, it just went that way.

She took a sip of her martini, then glanced to her left. Amira was there, looking regal, her long black hair flowing over her shoulders, her lovely breasts lovingly held in the décolletage of her dress, defining her femininity without screaming it. She wasn't wearing a bra, and looked chic without one.

The Omega Force dossier Svetlana had read about her was that she had been born in Lebanon, and that she had married David Marx, a wealthy man of uncertain means, when she was very young.

She's forty years old, and she looks sexier now than any twenty-year-old. The bitch.

Svetlana was well aware of the fact that her thought was spiteful without reason and catty beyond measure. It seemed she always got a little insecure about her looks when she was with Tatiana.

She mentally chastised herself, but not because she had such uncharitable thoughts. Partly because the thoughts were inappropriate when she was in the beginning of a mission, but mostly because they were unwarranted. When she had a job to do, Svetlana knew that she mustn't let anything distract her. To allow that to happen was to court disaster — and disaster was something that took the greatest pleasure in dishing out its nasty, sadistic revenge.

"They're a portal to a fountain of knowledge," Svetlana said to Tatiana, keeping her voice low. "What they know is what we need to know."

Tatiana nodded, and Svetlana tried hard to forget how erotic it had been to kiss her mouth. It was even harder to forget how erotic it had been to kiss all the other parts of her body, and the elicit thrill she had experienced when she felt Tatiana responding to her kisses. To hold Tatiana's ass cheeks in her hands as the teenager climaxed was something that Svetlana knew she would never forget.

But this wasn't the time to dwell on such thoughts, no matter how pleasant they might be.

Svetlana took a sip of her martini, looked at David and Amira, and gave them a smile that included both of them. She still wasn't certain how this assignment was supposed to be played, so she was holding her cards close to the vest.

In the next thirty minutes, two millionaires, three movies stars, and the son of a billionaire weapon's merchant approached Svetlana and Tatiana and tried to strike up a conversation. Svetlana would have none of it, though she did like the fact that they approached, because it gave her the chance to turn them away, and every time she did, she noted that David and Amira paid attention . . . and they seemed quite pleased that she was choosing to remain without any companionship other than the young woman she was with.

Svetlana had just ordered a second round of cocktails when

she saw Amira rise from her chair and head toward the ladies' restroom. She noted, with a critical eye, how swiftly the saloon's staff hurried to unlatch the thick, woven rope that sealed off the executive area from the rest of the nightclub.

Everywhere in the world, the staff understood who had money and power, and who only pretended to have it.

When Amira had risen from her chair, Svetlana said quickly to Tatiana, "Don't go anywhere."

Svetlana forced herself to not hurry when she followed Amira through the small opening that led to the general section of the nightclub. She walked into the bathroom only two steps behind Amira. When she inhaled, she caught the delicate scent of a perfume she could not identify, though she immediately experienced its evocative, very feminine allure.

The scent of it made Svetlana want to taste Amira.

Everywhere.

There were four stalls, and Svetlana was pleased that none of them had an occupant. Even though she didn't need to, Svetlana used a stall, then quickly came out. She was washing her hands when Amira came out. Svetlana smiled at her through the mirror as she finished washing her hands, then dried them with a paper towel that was dispensed with a motion sensor.

"If you'd like, you can sit with my husband and me," Amira said. "My name is Amira, and I've watched you fend off more men in the last thirty minutes than any beautiful woman should have to." She made an expression that Svetlana found utterly kissable. She wished she didn't, but she did—facts were facts, and that was just the way it was. "The young woman you're with is invited, of course. You can sit with my husband and me, and then maybe you can get some peace."

Svetlana smiled. "I think I'd like that very much."

She took a half-step closer to Amira. Svetlana could feel the sudden acceleration of her own heart, and she was aware that though she knew she was acting, there was a certain honesty to every word she spoke.

In a softer voice, Svetlana asked, "You're sure you wouldn't mind the intrusion? I wouldn't want to impose."

"It would be my pleasure," Amira said. "I promise you." She looked at Svetlana a bit more closely. "I don't recall seeing you here before."

"We don't come here often."

"We?"

"My sister and me."

"Oh," Amira said. She smiled, and she didn't turn her gaze away. "She's lovely. I'm sure that's why you protect her the way you do."

"I protect her?"

Amira smiled without breaking the visual connection she had with Svetlana. "Constantly. Though I certainly under-stand why. She's adorable." She smiled. "I'm Amira Marx. The gorgeous hunk of manhood at the table is my husband, David."

"I'm Svetlana Simonov, and that lovely girl at my table is my sister, Tatiana."

Svetlana looked at Amira's mouth, thinking that she might well possess the most kissable lips of any woman on the planet, when the bathroom door opened, and four women in their early twenties—and none of them even remotely so-ber—staggered into the bathroom, all of them talking over each other, and each one declaring that she had the most en-tertaining story that simply had to be listened to, so therefore, everyone else should stop talking.

The only thing that Svetlana was certain of was that she didn't have any interest in anything that any of them had to say.

There was some awkwardness when Amira and Svetlana

returned to their tables, but then everything was explained, and soon David, Amira, Svetlana, and Tatiana were seated around a single, small round table, all of them enjoying their libations as introductions were made and hands were shaken.

"So, you're new here," Amira said to Svetlana. "What brings you to town? Business?"

Svetlana shook her head. "Not this time. We're just relaxing and taking it easy for a while."

"What line of work are you in?" David asked.

Svetlana could tell that David was far more interested in her answer than just asking a casual question of a new acquaintance. She looked at him a moment without saying anything, as though she was deliberating just what her answer should be. Finally, she said, "I work for the family business. We're in the import-export business, for the most part. And you?"

David took a sip of his vodka before he replied, "International finance, mostly, though my wife and I also dabble in several other fields. More often than not we just introduce people who want to buy something to people who want to sell something."

"And take a pleasant percentage of the profits," Svetlana said, her smile utterly benign. "My family does that, too. Perhaps we know people that you'd like to meet, and vice versa."

"Yes. Quite likely. I'm sure I know people you'd like to meet."

Svetlana looked him directly in the eyes, though she said nothing for several seconds. It wasn't a challenging look, but rather an assessing one. And the way she looked at David was exactly the way he looked at her.

When David finally turned his gaze away, it was like he and Svetlana had come to an unspoken agreement of some sort. At that moment, Svetlana felt as though she had just achieved her first victory — albeit a minor one — of this mission.

After that there was small talk of inconsequential matters until an actor approached the table. Svetlana recognized him immediately, even though he hadn't made a movie in a half dozen years.

"I need to speak with you," the actor said, bending down toward David. Svetlana could see there was an anxious intensity in his eyes. Something was bothering him greatly. "Privately, if I could."

"I have guests," David said. There wasn't the slightest trace of respect in his tone. Anyone who heard him speak would know that. "Whatever you have to say will have to wait."

Svetlana touched the back of David's hand to draw his attention. She curled her fingers around his palm a moment later, and said, "My sister and I can go back to our table. When you're done with business, let us know and we'll come back." She gave his hand a firm squeeze that was somewhat more than just friendly. "I'd never forgive myself if I interfered with another person's business. Business before pleasure, right?" She put a certain inflection in the word *pleasure* that was impossible to miss.

Without waiting for a reply, Svetlana rose to her feet, then nodded to Tatiana, indicating they were to return to their original table. Without hesitation, Tatiana rose to her feet.

"I need that part," the actor said, sitting down in the chair that Svetlana had vacated. "It'll put me right back on top."

"That's what *you* need," David replied. "How does that affect what *I* need?"

"I'll give you twenty-five percent of my salary."

He made the statement as though he was being magnanimous. David despised him just a little bit more because of it. The man was an idiot, he just didn't know it.

"That's the cut your agent takes. You insult me by offering that. Besides, if your agent was such hot stuff, he'd have gotten you the part in that movie a long time ago. But he hasn't gotten you that part, just like he hasn't gotten you any movies in how long now? Six years? Seven?"

"How much do you want?"

After the actor asked the question, he closed his eyes. It was at that moment David knew he owned the actor's soul, and could do with it whatever he liked.

I'm God, and he knows it.

David would have smiled then at his self-awareness, but he had taught himself to keep his honest, innermost feelings to himself. Still, it was utterly satisfying to understand that one was God on Earth, with the power of life and death, of obscurity or fame. It was good to be God.

"Perhaps I could put a kind word in with the producer," David said, keeping his voice just loud enough to be heard above the music. "Maybe he'll listen to me, and maybe he won't."

David saw the hope suddenly shine in the actor's eyes. Everyone who had any sense listened to David when he spoke. To do otherwise was to court disaster. David knew that the actor knew that.

"If you . . . I'll never forget the favor you've done me," the actor said.

"But, of course, in exchange for my influence, you'll have to do something for me." David looked the actor directly in the eyes.

"Name it." The words came out of the actor's mouth with some hesitation. He was willing to do anything, give up anything, surrender everything, to get back onto the A-list of actors. But he couldn't give up his soul without some consideration.

"Of course, we mustn't forget the incident that got you blacklisted in the first place, can we? That's an obstacle I'll have to overcome before a producer with any standing in the industry is going to give you serious consideration."

David couldn't resist twisting the knife of truth in the actor's back. News of an orgy with girls who were overwhelmed by the actor's fame — and each with a nose full of cocaine that he had provided — had made the tabloids, and by the time it was on the Internet, there were photos to prove that the rumors were true. The actor had given a handful of girls in their late teens and early twenties enough cocaine to make them fuck a donkey if he told them to. The trouble was, some of them had their cell phones, and all of those phones had cameras.

After that, there wasn't a producer willing to talk to him, much less hire him. He was box office poison. Self-righteousness was reigning supreme. Especially among the least virtuous.

"You need me," David said quietly. "I need to hear you say that you need me."

He was twisting the knife in the actor's back even more, humbling him, and it felt so fucking good that David wanted to shout and do fist-pumps in the air. Instead, he looked the actor straight in the eyes, defying the once-great man to do anything other than supplicate himself on bended knee.

"I need you," the actor said. He closed his eyes. His subjugation was now complete, his humiliation absolute.

"If you want the role, I need two things."

The actor hesitated before saying, "Name them."

"I need fifty percent of your salary, along with fifty percent of any profit-sharing and residuals that come from the movie." David felt a tingling in his groin, just like he always did whenever he knew he was about to steal a man's soul. "And your wife. That lovely young woman you married. I'll need her for a week. Let's say we'll start next Friday. No, let's start next Saturday. She'll be available, won't she?"

36

The actor's voice had a tremor in it when he spoke. "My wife? Seriously?"

In a voice that was cold as the Arctic, David replied, "For a week. And she needn't pack anything other than lingerie for a seven days. She won't be leaving the bedroom."

"My wife?"

"And she does like satisfying women, doesn't she? My wife is ever so fond of young women who love to satisfy her passion. You're what? Forty-three? And your wife is twenty-three?"

"Twenty-four."

"I guess that'll have to do. I'll have my helicopter pick your wife up next Saturday. At the end of the week, if she's satisfactory, you'll get the role in that movie that'll put you on top again. If she's not satisfactory, then you'll continue to be blacklisted, and sooner rather than later, your beautiful, young wife will decide that she can do much better than you. Within weeks of figuring that out, she'll have hitched her wagon to another rich man, and you'll have neither a career, nor a beautiful wife."

CHAPTER FIVE

Aboard the *Corsair* off the coast of California

"Those sisters we met last night," Amira said, then grinned widely, "are not just sisters. And they're not just the daughters of a powerful man." She waited until her husband turned away from his computer before continuing. When he looked at her, she intentionally took a slow, deliberate sip of her morning coffee, keeping David waiting in suspense. "Our background check on Svetlana Simonov and her sister, Tatiana, was more than just a little interesting."

David's eyes narrowed as he said, "How so? And you've got a twinkle in your eyes that tells me I'm going to like what I'm about to hear."

"I put our computer geek on it, and he came up with one hell of a lot more information about those two than I thought he would." She half-sat on her husband's desk and looked down at him. There was a slow, simmering heat at the juncture of her thighs that had been teasing her since she had first read the report. The heat intensified when she watched the video that was attached to the report.

"Give me the details." David always liked to get the hard facts presented first, and lesser details dealt with later.

"In all likelihood, the Simonov girls are the illegitimate daughters of one of the founding members of the Russian Mafia."

David frowned. "That surprises me. I thought he was dead."

"That's the rumor, but nothing has been confirmed. And there have been stories of him being here, there, and everywhere. He's got the power and money to disappear if he wants to. Anyway, it sure as hell seems as though Svetlana and Tatiana grew up underground, since there wasn't a word about either of them regarding their early years. Then, suddenly, both are on the world scene, living the high life, staying in the finest hotels, living a life that takes a fortune to afford." Amira smiled wickedly. "Except they have no visible means of income. Everything they do gets paid for with credit cards. The bills go to a bank in the Bahamas, and then those bills get transferred to a bank in Switzerland, where they get paid. Everything gets paid. Thousand-dollar shoes. Designer dresses. You name it, and they not only can get it, it gets paid promptly, without question."

"Damn," David said softly. "The Russian Mafia? Do you know how much money we could make if we had a direct pipeline to the Russian Mafia?"

"That's what I've been calculating since I read the report. Christ, I get wet just thinking about the connections we could make. Those two ladies could be the biggest thing we've come across in years."

"Yes, they could."

"But there's more."

"Oh?"

"Let me drive, and I'll show you."

Amira waited until her husband got out of his chair, then she stepped around the desk and sat in front of his computer. She was distinctly aware of the scissoring of her thighs when she walked, and of the gentle but insistent throb in her vagina with each move she made. Her nipples, even though they weren't being caressed, were slightly peaked, and they were much more sensitive than usual. She was shockingly aware of every part of her body.

She made the necessary keystrokes, and the dark web came onto the screen. The words "Svetlana Simonov and her sister, Tatiana" flashed in vivid blood red letters against a black background.

"You're not going to believe this," Amira said in a voice that was suddenly husky with passion.

David moved so that he was standing beside her chair. Amira could feel his presence, even though she was staring at the computer monitor with unblinking eyes. She had already watched the twelve-minute video three times. The first time she had simply watched it. The second time she had masturbated while watching it. The third time she watched it, she climaxed twice while finger-fucking herself. She would have watched it a fourth time, but the uncomfortable, nasty sharp edge to her lust had been dulled sufficiently with her climaxes that she decided her husband should probably be let in on the fun.

It seemed a fair thing to do, and she tried to be fair with her life partner who always found her such entertaining people to have sex with.

For the next twelve minutes, neither David nor Amira said a word as they watched Svetlana and Tatiana first making love with each other, and then with a man whose face was never seen.

"This is revenge," Amira said. "Whoever the hell that guy is, he's the one who released this onto the Internet."

"If their father really is one of the founding members of the Russian Mafia, then that guy on the video with the big cock better find a hole to hide in, because Daddy's going to want revenge, and the Russian Mafia isn't known for their forgiving nature."

"Let me sit in the chair," David said. "Let's watch it again."

Amira got out of the chair, and as she did, she looked at her husband's crotch. His trousers were bulging. The urge to drop to her knees in front of him was almost overwhelming.

"I'll get it started again," David said, but before he sat in the chair in front of his computer, he opened his trousers and pushed them and his underwear down to his knees. Then he sat with his erection pointed straight up.

"They're sisters," Amira said as she tugged her panties down her legs, then stepped out of them. "Sisters." She straddled her husband's thighs, then reached down to guide the crown of his cock to her moist entrance. "We've got to fuck them. Both of them."

"One at a time," David said as Amira felt the head of his cock separating the lips of her pussy, "or both at the same time?"

"One at a time to begin with," Amira said as she lowered her hips slowly, shivering as her husband's cock began filling her tight channel. "Then both of them together."

"And it's the younger one that makes your pussy so wet, isn't it?"

"Yes," Amira replied honestly. "So's so young . . . and I'm forty."

"You'll have her," David said. "I promise you that. You'll taste that young pussy."

Los Angeles, California

The knock at the hotel door roused Tatiana. She was sitting in an overstuffed chair, and though she had been reading earlier, now she was napping. The previous evening had gone on very long, and after the excitement of meeting David and Amira, when she returned to her room, she found it impossible to sleep.

Before answering the door, Tatiana checked her appearance in the mirror. She decided that there was nothing wrong with her makeup, and her light tank top and casual cotton shorts were nothing to draw anyone's undue attention.

When she opened the door, she found an elderly man in livery. He was holding a silver tray, and on it was a small, rectangular envelope. On the envelope, in black ink in formal handwriting, was, "Svetlana and Tatiana Simonov."

"For you, miss," the elderly bellboy said, holding the tray out.

Tatiana took the envelope, but resisted the urge to tear it open immediately.

"Please wait," she said. "I have to give you a tip."

"That's not necessary, miss."

She looked him in the eyes and said with quiet authority, "It most certainly is."

She went to her purse and extracted two twenty-dollar bills. When she handed them to the man, she saw his eyes widen, and she knew that he wasn't accustomed to getting such generous tips. It made her all the happier that she had done what she'd done.

"Thank you," she said, then closed the door.

She hurried back to the overstuffed chair she had been napping in, sat down, and ripped open the envelope.

It was a woman's handwriting, and it was done so excellently that Tatiana wondered for a moment whether it was actually a computer font that had created the words.

"It would please us enormously if you would come to spend the day on our boat. We so enjoyed our time with you last night. Sincerely, David and Amira."

A shiver of anticipation went through Tatiana. This was *exactly* what Svetlana had said she wanted to have happen. It was the first step in getting into the cloistered inner circle of protection that the politicians had barricaded themselves behind.

"Svetlana, I think you're going to want to read this,"

Tatiana said. She heard the shower being turned off.

"Is anything wrong?" Svetlana asked from behind the door.

"Quite the opposite."

Standing on the rooftop of the hotel, near the heliport, Svetlana watched the approaching helicopter and tried to tamp down her rising excitement. When she had taken the assignment from Burke, she'd had little idea of how she was supposed to proceed. Her usual *modus operandi* for defeating an enemy was to kill him, usually with explosives, but sometimes with bullets. This time it was different. She had to destroy two men without making it obvious that that was what she had set out to do.

But it's all coming together.

Svetlana looked to her right. Tatiana was standing there, looking at the approaching helicopter with a sense of wonder in her expression.

She's learning so much. And she's learning it so fast.

It was a comforting thought for Svetlana. She hadn't wanted to work with any partner, much less one that had so little experience, but she couldn't find any fault with either Tatiana's skills, or, even more importantly, her ability to adapt and adjust to new situations accordingly.

The helicopter landed smoothly, smack in the center of the white circle on the rooftop of the hotel. The instant the landing skids were on the rooftop, the right door opened, and a smiling man in an immaculate gray suit and the look of a bodyguard about him stepped out and hurried forward.

"Good afternoon," he said. "I hope I didn't keep you waiting."

The helicopter had arrived precisely on time, and both Svetlana and the hired man knew it. Svetlana smiled at him. She wondered what kind of gun he carried.

"Not to worry," she said, having to raise her voice above

the sound of the churning helicopter blades. "How long will the ride take? I'm not real fond of being in the air."

"Mr. and Mrs. Marx's boat is fourteen miles out to sea. It won't take long, but I'll tell the pilot to make sure we get us there in a hurry."

"It's okay to be in a hurry, but it's more important to be safe," Svetlana said with honesty. She was exaggerating her fear of flying, but only by a little. She was a firm believer in the concept that if God had meant man to fly, He would have given them wings.

"Don't you worry about a thing. Mr. and Mrs. Marx have taken care of everything." He looked into Svetlana's eyes for a moment, then said, "They always do."

Svetlana felt a shiver go through her, though she couldn't say why.

Aboard the *Corsair* on the Pacific Ocean

Her world was spinning smoothly, and that was always a comforting thing for Amira to realize. Her husband was the mastermind of the operation, the one who came up with all the best ideas, and Amira had long ago learned to accept that. But she was the one who saw David's ideas through to fruition. She was the one who always made sure that a good idea eventually had a good outcome. She didn't flit from one idea to the next without ever looking back. She was the one in the marriage who made sure that at the end of the day, David's brilliant ideas meant money in the bank.

Because, after all, it was only the money in the bank that mattered. Everything else was just useless talk and empty bullshit.

There was a soft knock on her door, and Amira called out, "Yes?"

The door opened, but not completely. Just a few inches. The crewmen all knew that Mrs. Marx might or might not have clothes on, and they were all smart enough to realize that if she wanted to be looked at when she was naked, then she'd be on deck, out in the open where everyone could see her as she sunbathed in the nude. That had happened, but usually not unless she started her day with Bloody Marys.

"Madam, the helicopter is returning," the crewman said. "You asked that I inform you before it lands."

"Yes, I did," Amira replied. She tried to remember the crewman's name, couldn't, then dismissed the issue. Whoever he was, he was replaceable in Amira's life. All she had to do was ask her husband to have him thrown overboard, and a minute later he'd be in the water more than a dozen miles from shore, and quietly likely soon to be a shark's supper. "Thank you," Amira said, remembering that she should maintain at least the appearance of politeness with the hired help. "You can go now."

"Yes, ma'am," the crewman said, then closed the door.

Tatiana's coming here.

The thought sent a thrill through Amira. The first time she'd seen Tatiana, she had thought her the loveliest young woman she'd ever seen. After Amira had drunk a couple glasses of champagne in the nightclub the previous night, when she looked at Tatiana, she became quite convinced that she was the loveliest young woman ever to walk the planet. And Tatiana probably had the most delicious pussy the world had ever known. Amira was quite convinced of this.

Once she's on board, there's no way for her to get off without the helicopter or the motor cruiser. Amira smiled in a feline, carnivorous manner. *She's young and naïve and when she eats my pussy, she probably won't be very good at it since she's probably never been with a woman other than her sister before. That's okay. I'll be her tutor. I'll teach her everything she needs to know.*

There was always something special for Amira about being

a young woman's *first*, or at least very nearly the first. The conquest, the deflowering, was always so much sweeter when Amira knew with certainty that she was in territory that no other woman had ever been. She didn't really care if the girl had been with other men, since men other than her husband meant nothing to her. But if she was the first woman a girl had been with, then that made the seduction all the more satisfying.

She inhaled deeply through her nostrils, let her breath out slowly through her lips, then stepped out of the yacht's stateroom and prepared to meet the guests.

This is utter chaos. This is Sodom and Gomorrah on a multi-million-dollar yacht.

Svetlana was actually amused by all the things that were going on around her. Since getting off the helicopter onto David and Amira's yacht, she had watched the kind of behavior that would have made the ancient Romans blush with shame. On the deck were perhaps ten or twelve men and approximately twice that many young women. The men were in their forties or fifties, and the women in their twenties. All the women were attractive and wearing string bikinis that put their beautiful bodies on display. The men were mostly wearing khaki shorts with polo shirts, all of them looking like they had just gotten into their casual clothes after having left an executive board meeting. The men were the movers and shakers of American industry, and the women were the entertainment that kept the men happy while they were out to sea and away from their wives.

"Are any or all of these men married?" Svetlana asked David.

"Most of them are married," David replied. "That's why your cell phone was confiscated when you arrived. There's nobody here who wants any photographic evidence that he was ever here." He smiled at her. "On this boat, privacy is a guarantee."

"I thought as much," Svetlana replied. "Is it always like this?" She made a vague gesture toward two men who were making out with women half their age.

"Most times," David replied with a smile. "My wife and I like to surround ourselves with the most interesting and entertaining people on the planet. These people are all interesting or entertaining."

"Certainly the most beautiful," she said, indicating with her champagne glass several young women who were nothing less than absolutely gorgeous, and each of them wearing a string bikini that barely covered the essentials. "And powerful, I'd imagine."

"Yes. Beautiful and powerful. A lovely combination, don't you think?"

"Yes," Svetlana replied. "Yes. Quite."

"Perhaps this is the right time for you and me to go down to my office, where we can talk quietly, and with privacy," David said. "Would you like that? Whatever you want, I can provide."

I'll bet you can. Svetlana followed David as he led her away from the carnival atmosphere of the main deck, down two flights of stairs, then down a long hallway.

"This is my office," David said, opening a door. "This is where I make the money that pays for the non-stop party going on the main deck."

He opened the door wide, then stepped aside so that Svetlana could enter first. Svetlana could tell that he was showing off, but when she looked at his office, with the enormous cherry wood desk, the leather furniture, the extra-large windows that gave him a view of the endless ocean, she could understand why he was proud of it.

"Stunning," Svetlana said honestly, standing in the

doorway. "Beautiful."

The entire far wall was ankle-to-ceiling glass. On the inner walls, there were portraits and pictures of David and Amira. Svetlana noted that none of the pictures were of David alone. Amira was always with him, and Svetlana made a point of remembering that. David and Amira weren't just husband and wife, and they weren't just business partners — they were a team, two halves of a single whole. There was not one without the other.

In some ways, Svetlana envied David for the relationship he had with his partner in life.

"Please, have a seat," David said. "Is there anything I can get you?"

"Not just yet, but thank you," Svetlana replied. Actually, she wanted another glass of the exquisite champagne very much, but this wasn't the time to overindulge. She looked around the yacht's private office and said with quiet sincerity, "I can see why you love it here. This is heaven on earth." She chuckled. "Or at least heaven on water."

"Yes," David replied. He sat in an overstuffed, leather easy chair. "That's exactly the way I see it. That was my intention from the very beginning."

Svetlana sat in a chair near David, crossed her legs at the knee, took a sip of her champagne, and said, "So, my dear Mr. Marx, it seems you know a great deal of people who have influence in this world. Coincidentally, so do I. What do you think the odds are that you know people I want to meet, and that I know people you want to meet? And somehow, some way, we can both turn a profit by knowing the right people."

Svetlana saw a sudden gleam come into David's eyes, and she knew that she had played her cards exactly right.

She felt a thrill that was almost sexual in nature.

CHAPTER SIX

"It seems we're always entertaining," Amira said, waving with her champagne glass toward the yacht's main-deck hot tub, where middle-aged men of clearly significant means were trying to remove the top half of bikinis from seven young women. For the most part, the men seemed to be succeeding. "Sometimes I find it amusing, though to be honest, I find it less and less interesting as times marches on."

"This is a big boat," Tatiana replied. "Let's find somewhere else to talk."

Amira flinched, though only for a second, and she wondered whether Tatiana had said exactly the right thing, or just the opposite.

"I don't care where you take me," Tatiana said softly, "but I want to be in the sun, and I want to have some privacy. Is that asking too much?"

Amira shook her head. "That's not asking too much. That's just asking for exactly what I want myself right now."

To get to the starboard observation deck, they had to go through the interior of the yacht. As they walked from the glaring sunlight to the dark hallway, Tatiana stumbled slightly.

Amira immediately took her hand. "I have you," she said, squeezing Tatiana's hand just a little more tightly. She could hear the undercurrent in her own tone when she said, "Just follow me. I'll take you wherever you want to go."

If she doesn't want to kiss me, I'll be the most disappointed woman on the planet.

When this thought went through her brain, Amira flinched sharply, as though she had been given an electrical shock. She'd always thought that if ever there was a coldly logical, rational woman on the planet, then she was that person. But with Tatiana, she found herself intellectually and emotionally drifting into areas that had nothing to do with logic and reason.

She squeezed her fingers a bit more tightly around Tatiana's hand as she guided her through the room and then out onto the starboard balcony. They were alone on the twelve-by-twelve-foot section of the boat, and for that, Amira was thankful.

For a moment she deliberated whether she should give orders to the crew that she wasn't to be disturbed, but she discounted this almost immediately. If her husband discovered that she didn't want to be disturbed, then the first thing he would do would be to show up, and that was the last thing that she wanted just then.

His big cock was lovely, satisfying, and delicious . . . and it was the last thing she was in the mood for when Tatiana was blinking her eyes as she stepped out into the brilliant sunlight looking as though she had never, ever been on her knees in front of a woman to give cunnilingus. Amira knew that she had.

Memories of the video Amira had watched of Tatiana with her older sister were never far from her awareness. Watching the video of them making love was the single most erotic thing that Amira had ever seen in her life.

If she doesn't lick my pussy, there is no God in heaven.

Amira knew she shouldn't think such things, but this didn't make her stop thinking them.

"Is there anything you'd like?" Amira asked as they stepped out into the sunshine.

Like maybe oral sex until you beg me to stop because you've come so many times that you just can't stand the thought of coming again?

Amira squeezed her eyes tightly closed for several seconds, and demanded of herself that she not think such things ever again. At least not when she was alone with Tatiana and the girl was looking as ripe and juicy as a freshly cut piece of watermelon that was just waiting to be devoured.

Like one of Pavlov's dogs, when Amira had the thought of devouring Tatiana, her mouth began to salivate.

I'd go down on her for days without end. When she finally begged me to stop, she wouldn't remember how many times I'd made her come.

"This is beautiful," Tatiana said, looking at the ocean.

The simple, artless comment drew Amira out of her own reverie and brought her back to the present. She looked at Tatiana and smiled, hoping that her own rampaging lust wasn't obvious in her body language and expression.

"Yes," Amira said, her voice much softer now that there wasn't the cacophony of more than a dozen people above her. "I love this part of the boat. It's the one place that's truly private."

Amira felt her heart suddenly seize up in her chest when Tatiana turned toward her quickly and said, "Really? You only have privacy when you're here?" The girl blushed then, and said, "I'm honored. I get the feeling that you're treating me to an experience that most visitors don't get."

If she doesn't eat my pussy, there's no reason for living.

Amira said, "Yes, that's right. Almost everywhere on the boat, there are crewmen or guests. But here, I'm alone. So, for now, it's just you and me."

Amira was not a patient woman, but she also knew that sometimes a delayed reward made the final payoff so much sweeter. The urge to pounce upon Tatiana was very strong, but she also knew that to give in to her baser instincts would not deliver her the end results that she now desperately wanted.

"Can I get you another drink?" Amira asked, keeping her tone just as sweet as honey itself. After several seconds, she added, "I can give you anything you want."

The underlying meaning could not be either ignored or dismissed. When Tatiana looked into her eyes, Amira knew that her point had been made, and that Tatiana had understood not only what had been said, but also what had *not* been said.

Amira felt her pussy clench at the possibilities of what might soon happen. She couldn't conceive of a situation where she wouldn't climax. Frequently.

It was at times like these—and they didn't happen very often—when Amira was tempted to break the promise that she had made with David so many years ago. She had never violated that oath, and she was absolutely certain that her husband hadn't, either. The vow was a simple one, but it was iron-clad. There could be no men other than David in their sex life. However, since Amira liked to occasionally indulge herself with women, that would be entirely permissible so long as certain rules were followed. Namely, Amira could not have sex with a woman unless David was there to watch the activities. If the new woman was willing to have sex with David, that was entirely within the rules, but Amira got to watch, and possibly even participate. But under no circumstances was Amira allowed to seduce a woman unless David was there to witness all the libidinous action, and if David seduced the same woman, Amira was not allowed to in any way be jealous of the sexual encounter.

It was parameters they had lived by for many years, and through many shared lovers.

I've never had sex with two sisters at the same time. I've never even thought of it until I saw the video of Svetlana and Tatiana together.

Of all the things in the sexual realm that Amira and David had done together, bedding sisters was something entirely new—and thoroughly arousing. Amira's panties got wet just thinking about the possibilities.

Tatiana stood at the balcony's railing, looking out at the blue water, her blonde hair swirling gently against her cheeks and shoulders. Looking at her in profile, Amira was certain that she had never seen a more lovingly innocent young woman in her life.

She looks virginal, but she has sex with her sister, and her sister's boyfriend. Or at least her ex-boyfriend.

Amira liked the thought. When she seduced Tatiana, and then turned her over to David, it wouldn't be as though she was deflowering a virgin. But still, it was a particularly erotic thrill to see such young beauty.

I'll bet she's never tasted pussy other than her own sister's. That would explain how she maintains such a sweet outward appearance. She's got one persona for the bedroom, and one for the outside world.

The idea of being Tatiana's new lover made her shiver. The idea of being both Tatiana's and Svetlana's new lover — and having them both at the same time — made her tremble.

It had been a long time since Amira trembled for anyone but her husband.

"It's good to have you here," Amira said, moving so that she stood beside Tatiana at the railing. "We get so few fresh faces."

"It's good to be here," Tatiana replied. "I love being on the water. I always have. Even when I was just a little girl, I always loved being on board a boat."

"Is there anything I can get you? Anything you'd like to eat or drink? We have an excellent chef aboard, and up one floor we have a fully stocked bar."

Tatiana shook her head.

What would she do if I brought her to the Dungeon?

Another shiver went through Amira at the thought of taking Tatiana to the infamous Dungeon in the bowels of the yacht. It was a large dark room with mattresses on the floor from wall to wall, countless pillows, and most infamously of all, various bondage devices to cater to those who felt inclined to indulge in such pleasures.

In the darkest corner of her mind, Amira envisioned herself giving commands that Tatiana would have to follow. First she'd make the girl strip—and do it very slowly. Then she'd tie Tatiana's hands behind her back with a velvet rope, then put another rope around her ankles. What would come after that? Forcing her to her knees to perform oral sex for an hour straight? Or what about taking a riding crop to the pale, firm cheeks of her ass?

Amira felt a charge of lustful electricity go through her veins, then go straight to her vagina. She had put other women in bondage, and had forced them to give her pleasure, but none in her past could compare to Tatiana's allure. She was the ultimate combination of youthful innocence and wanton taboo excess.

To look at her, you'd think she was still a virgin.

But playing almost endlessly in Amira's head, and in her libido, was the video of Tatiana with her sister and the faceless man with the very large cock. Amira couldn't forget about the obvious satisfaction that Tatiana had taken when she was sucking on Svetlana's breasts, and later, sucking on the man's hard cock.

Hoping she didn't sound like she was prying, Amira said, "So tell me a little bit about yourself. Is there a boyfriend in your life?"

"I'm afraid not."

Amira's mouth suddenly felt very dry. "What about a girlfriend?"

"No. Not one of those, either."

Then it's just you with your sister and her ex-boyfriend. Since Tatiana wasn't looking at her, Amira allowed herself to smile. *I think your sex life is about to get a lot more complicated.*

"I've been looking for someone who has political influence here in the United States," Svetlana said, leaning back just a little in the overstuffed chair in David's office. "There are certain things my family corporation needs—variances, and so forth—that require governmental assistance. You know, help with cutting through the red tape, the bureaucracy, and all the paperwork."

"Yes," David replied, his emotions soaring because that was precisely what he had hoped Svetlana would say. "I know exactly what you're talking about, and I know people who might be able to help you."

Though her dress came down to the tops of her knees, with her legs now crossed, he was given a mouthwatering view of creamy, tapering thighs, and David could imagine the ecstasy that would be his when he felt those naked thighs surrounding his hips.

David felt his always-responsive cock start to twitch inside his trousers, and with effort, he forced himself to concentrate of Svetlana's words and not her body.

"I know some people in politics," David said after some deliberation. "Perhaps you'd like to meet them? They're coming here on Friday."

"That's just the day after next," Svetlana replied.

David saw a bright light come into Svetlana's blue eyes. He knew she wasn't just *interested* in meeting people in government, she was practically *desperate* to meet them.

I've got you now. You need me for introductions, and because you need me, I own you.

He smiled at the thought of having control over Svetlana and Tatiana. Power over women was, for David, the ultimate aphrodisiac. His cock always turned to stone whenever he knew that the woman had no real choice but to relent to his passion, to succumb to his lust, to do whatever he demanded of her, and do it without complaint.

I'm going to fuck you and your sister, and so is my wife.

"You don't mind staying here on the boat until then?" David asked.

"I'll have to get my things from the hotel first."

David made a dismissive motion with his hand. "I can send for them."

"But—"

"Let me take care of everything." He spoke with the confidence of a man who could, in point of fact, take care of everything. "While you're here you can just relax and enjoy yourself."

"You're sure it's not too much of a bother?"

David let his gaze go from her face down to her breasts. Though she was showing only a modest amount of cleavage, David remembered what her naked breasts had looked like on the video, and how she had moaned with passion when Tatiana had sucked on her nipples.

"Don't worry about a thing. Amira and I will take care of everything."

CHAPTER SEVEN

Washington, D.C.

Congressman Norman Todd looked at his wristwatch and tried to keep from yawning. He was into the third hour of a special committee meeting, and the truth of it was, he didn't give a damn about what was being said or what was being decided on. He had already gotten the information he needed regarding the new surface-to-air missiles the military was developing, and he'd already sold that information for a small fortune that had been deposited into his Jamaican bank account.

Tomorrow I get on a plane, and shortly after landing at LAX I'll be aboard the Corsair. *I'll drink my whiskey on the rocks and get my rocks off with a little cutie I haven't met yet.*

The chance encounter he'd had two years earlier with David and Amira Marx had turned his entire life around. After meeting them he suddenly got the campaign contributions that he desperately needed for reelection, and it wasn't long after that he was given a prime role on a Congressional committee that oversaw military spending and weapons development. And shortly after that, David introduced him to Sun Ming Po, and after pleasantries were exchanged and confidence and trust were built, money started flowing into Todd's newly-created Jamaican bank account, and top secret information made its way from Todd to Sun Ming Po.

Todd looked around the room. He knew everyone in the room, just as he knew which ones didn't really give a shit about their constituents, and which ones were fucking around on their spouses. But they didn't know much about him. They knew he had a wife who was continuing to gain weight, and that he had two kids who were still in school, but academically not doing well. What they didn't know was that he had a sex life that would put a sheik with a billion dollars in the bank from oil to shame. Once a month, Todd stayed aboard the *Corsair* for two or three days, and he usually had at least one new girl a day. Sometimes he had them two at the same time, though it seemed to him that Amira thought that was being a bit greedy on his part. He tried to keep his *ménage a trois* appetite held in check. It wouldn't do to get Amira angry. She and David were the gatekeepers to a life of hedonistic sexual excess and a Midas-like fortune in gold that neither the IRS nor his wife knew anything about.

Todd would leave Friday morning and not be back in Washington D.C. until Sunday night. During the hours in between, he'd either be fucking a girl half his age, or he'd be drinking whiskey that was twelve years old.

Either way, he'd be in heaven.

Washington D.C.

Senator Arthur Conrad sat in his office in the Russell Senate Building and resisted the urge to open his desk drawer, take out the small bottle of very expensive London dry gin, and savor a small shot of the delicious libation. The gin was the reason he always kept a bowl of peppermint candies on his desk. On the breath, there was no difference between peppermint and gin.

When he noticed the green light on his intercom phone, he touched a button and said, "Yes, J.J.?"

"Just a reminder, sir, that you're scheduled for a conference call in fifteen minutes," his secretary said.

Conrad smiled to himself. His secretary, a handsome young man in his middle twenties, was discreetly gay, terribly loyal, made sure that Conrad was always where he was supposed to be, and was familiar with the reports that he was supposed to read but usually didn't. The secretary had started out as an intern but had worked his way into a full-time position on Conrad's staff.

Conrad didn't care that his secretary was gay, so long as he always arranged Conrad's commitments in such a manner that the press and his constituents all believed with certainty that Conrad was a hard-working public servant who was faithful to his wife and children.

Nothing could be further from the truth, but Conrad didn't mind at all being a world-class hypocrite. Not when he had money in a Jamaican numbered bank account and a seemingly limitless supply of young women who were only too happy to satisfy his lusty urges, no matter how kinky they were.

It had all started when he'd met David and Amira Marx, and they had casually wondered whether or not he'd like to relax aboard their yacht, the *Corsair*.

"It might be nice to get away from the cameras and relax," he had said, not realizing that he had just changed his life forever.

"Trust me," David said, "When you're aboard the *Corsair*, there won't be any cameras to worry about."

And David was true to his word. The first time Conrad was flown via helicopter to the yacht, he was wanded by a security guard with a metal detector. His phone was put into a zippered plastic bag, along with his wallet. It wasn't long before a young woman was removing Conrad's necktie, then suitcoat, and wing-tipped shoes. A couple cocktails after that, a different young woman was unbuckling his belt, unbuttoning his shirt, and sucking on his nipples.

One hour and one orgasm later, Conrad was quite convinced that if there was a heaven on earth, then it had to be found aboard the *Corsair*, in the Dungeon.

But the day got even better. While still wallowing in post-orgasmic bliss, Conrad was introduced by David and Amira to Sun Ming Po, where it was explained that in exchange for some top secret information regarding submarine deployment, Conrad would become a very wealthy senator.

Conrad's only real concern was that he not get caught. He didn't give a rat's ass about giving an enemy information that could be used against the United States. In fact, that wasn't even a consideration. All Conrad was really concerned about was whether he would get caught and whether he had access anywhere in the world to the vast fortune in cash that he was about to sell out his country for.

I might be a traitor, but at least I'm not a cut-rate traitor.

He let his mind wander as a senator from a neighboring state stepped up to the podium. Conrad thought about the petite girl he'd enjoyed the last time he was aboard the *Corsair*. She had liked it when he put the fur-lined handcuffs on her, and after he ravaged her, she liked it that he used a mink glove to smooth away the red marks on her back that had been caused by his leather belt.

He wondered if she'd be there when he got to the *Corsair* on Friday. He hoped so, but if not, there would be someone else.

Aboard the *Corsair*, on the Pacific Ocean

"So, what do you think?" David asked, sitting behind his desk.

"Is your question regarding business or sex?" Amira asked as she sat on the long sofa in the office.

"Let's say it involves both."

"As for business, I couldn't really tell how much she knows. I got the impression that if there's going to be a business angle to our relations with them, then we'll have to concentrate on Svetlana. As for sex, Tatiana didn't let anything out. She presents herself pretty much as an innocent, but you and I both know that she's not."

The video images of Svetlana and Tatiana having sex were seared into David's brain, and would remain there his entire life. He was certain of that.

"I suspect that with some effort on our part, we can both have a very good time with her," Amira said. "What did you pick up from Svetlana?"

"She is in need of political influence, and she's probably covering for her father, who I'm more convinced than ever is who we think he is. I believe he's still alive, and is still a leader of the Russian Mafia." He lifted his eyebrows briefly, giving his wife a boyish smile. "Siblings. That'll be a new one for us, won't it?"

"I've been getting bored with those empty-headed twits we've had lately," Amira replied. "They're young and sexy and might satisfy silly old rich white men, but you and I should set for ourselves a higher standard."

"Do you think we can get them to the Dungeon?"

This time it was Amira's turn to smile impishly. "You're going to like doing it with Tatiana. My guess is that she was initiated by her sister, and that's all she's ever been with. Big sister seduces her, and now protects her from everyone else." She closed her eyes briefly. "Fuck, that's erotic to think about."

"Yes, it is. It damned sure is."

"Did you learn anything?" Svetlana asked Tatiana as they

stood in their room aboard the *Corsair*.

"She asks more questions than she gives answers," Tatiana replied. "I get the feeling that she and her husband have an equal partnership." She smiled a bit sheepishly, then shrugged her slender shoulders. "I'm pretty sure she wants to have sex with me."

Who in hell wouldn't want to have sex with you? "Well, that's probably a very good sign," Svetlana said, trying to dismiss entirely the previous thought, which she had shown the good sense to keep unspoken. "We've got to keep them amused with our presence until Friday, then we'll get them to make the introductions so that Congressman Todd and Senator Conrad, will trust us." She looked at the assortment of string bikinis that were strewn on the bed. Amira had provided them. "An introduction from David and Amira means every-thing. It's the only way those traitors will trust us enough to let their guard down."

"Did you want to get some sun, or should we just walk around for a while?"

Svetlana considered her options, not entirely certain she wanted to walk around the yacht wearing only a very small, very sheer bikini with so many complete strangers aboard. Besides, since it was obvious that the women aboard the yacht were there by invitation so they could entertain the men, she didn't want the men to think she was available.

"David said he had a ninety-minute phone call that he simply couldn't miss or postpone," Svetlana answered. "Why don't you get some sun? I'll mingle with the other guests and see if I can pick up anything."

Svetlana watched the men all turn their heads to follow Tatiana's progress as she walked past the hot tub and went to the small portable bar where a bartender was making potent cocktails and dispensing cold cans of beer. Tatiana, blonde and pale-skinned, had chosen as counterpoint a navy-blue string bikini top and bottom which contrasted nicely with her complexion. Her breasts were gently held in triangular cups that were large enough to hold them completely. The bottom half of her bikini was small in back, and very small in front.

It's a good thing she had a full-body wax before we started this assignment.

Svetlana, leaning back against the guard railing near the stern of the yacht, had spent the past hour and a half talking with middle-aged men who possessed money and power, and women younger than herself who she suspected had neither money nor power but wanted access to both. The young women weren't for sale, and they weren't even openly venal. They just wanted to improve their financial lot in life, and being young and beautiful was a way for them to do exactly that. Svetlana suspected Amira had been the one to explain that to them.

Svetlana noticed David and Amira stepping up onto the deck. Instead of looking at them, she looked at the other guests, and she was only a little surprised at the reaction the host and hostess of the never-ending party drew. The men looked at them cautiously, and seemed to be making a point of not staring too lustfully at Amira. But it was the young women whose reaction to David and Amira surprised her. Almost to a person they seemed to look at the two covetously, with a strange mixture of desire, envy, and hope.

David and Amira can open the doors that these young women want to walk through. Doors that are now closed to them, and which they could never unlock on their own. They need David and Amira if they're ever going to take the next step up on the financial ladder.

Svetlana watched as David and Amira saw Tatiana in her revealing bikini. When they first looked at her, both of them stopped walking, and they then exchanged a look that said without words they both liked what they were looking at.

Svetlana felt a knife-stab of emotion go through her,

suddenly feeling that she wasn't sexy enough for the assignment she'd been given by Omega Force, and that an eighteen-year-old who not long ago had been in boot camp had played a trump card that Svetlana no longer held in her hands.

David and Amira walked up to Svetlana. They were still dressed in business attire, as was Svetlana, though everyone else on deck was in casual clothes, or a string bikini like the one Tatiana was wearing.

"I hope you didn't find this party too boring during my absence," David said, looking Svetlana directly in the eyes. "Some of my guests are very interesting. Others, I'm afraid, are not." He shrugged his shoulders. "As long as they're happy, then I'm happy."

"The perfect host." Svetlana understood that influence peddling came with many rewards, but it also came with a price. She turned to Amira, looked directly into her chocolate brown eyes, and added in a voice that was softer, but distinctly more sultry, "And, of course, the *perfect* hostess."

She saw the immediate reaction from Amira to being complimented, and she sensed she had made the right move. If David and Amira really were the soulmates that Svetlana and Tatiana thought they were, then the best way to get inside their inner circle was to appeal to both of them.

"I'm not perfect," Amira said, her voice also carrying an undercurrent of sensuality to it, "but I always try to be. Especially for . . ."

She left the final word unspoken, and because she had, she interested Svetlana so much more. She understood that Amira was playing her, but she also believed that there was an honesty about Amira that she had not at first realized. Suddenly, Svetlana didn't feel quite so unattractive as she had when she first saw the men and women reacting to Tatiana in a revealing bikini.

"Trust me," Svetlana said, her gaze unwavering from

Amira's, "you're perfect."

Amira smiled, then said quietly, "Well, I certainly try to be."

The day was wearing on, and the guests had been drinking since noon. Though there were many young women on deck, all of them wearing a bikini — the one-size-fits-all variety that David and his wife had provided — so there was plenty of skin to be seen. But David couldn't find any pleasure in seeing all the young women. The only one that drew his gaze and fired up his libido, was the young woman sitting beside him on the foredeck with a glass of champagne in her hand. The sheer nylon material of her bikini enabled the shape of her nipples to be seen. David tried telling himself that at the age of fifty, and with more sexual conquests to his name than he could count, he didn't have to stare at her nipples. But doing anything other than staring like a schoolboy at Tatiana was damned near impossible. She was, as his wife had explained, the ultimate combination of virginal innocence and taboo experience.

She goes down on her own sister's pussy, then blushes when I say the most harmless, off-color joke. She's everything in the extreme.

Sensing that he would very soon have a raging erection that he didn't want to have to hide or explain away, David turned his attention toward Svetlana — but when he did, the enticement to getting an erection was no less powerful. Svetlana was looking at Amira, so David could see her in perfect profile. The features of her face — the forehead, nose, mouth, and all that perfectly coiffured blonde hair — were the things that sculptures were modeled after. When he looked at her lips, he thought them to be the most kissable lips in the world — with the singular exception of his wife.

In everything, Amira always came first. But Svetlana came

a close second.

If her father really is a czar with the Russian Mafia, I'll make millions just knowing his daughter.

It was a heady thought. David was already worth a billion dollars, but the one thing that every billionaire wanted was the next billion. And David was no different in that aspect than any other wealthy man.

David watched as one of the businessmen he'd invited to the yacht took the hands of two young women and headed off to the stairway that led down to the Dungeon. The man was big into American-made steel, and he had paid David a small fortune to get tariffs put on foreign-made steel. He also knew that the businessman had a propensity to climax very quickly, especially if he was sober. Several of the young women that he'd been with in the Dungeon had told David as much.

He's trying to do two at once? What an idiot. He'll be back in the hot tub with empty balls and a limp dick inside ten minutes.

It was precisely ten minutes later that the businessman, looking as though someone had stolen the wind from his sales, returned to the deck of the *Corsair*.

David was impressed with his own powers of observation, and entirely unimpressed with the businessman's sexual prowess.

A few moments later, both young women who had gone down to the Dungeon stepped closer to David. They stayed far enough away so that they wouldn't directly intrude on David's conversation with Svetlana, but they made their presence known.

David ended his conversation and approached the two young women. He put a hand on their shoulders, enjoying the contact of their young flesh against his palms.

"What is it?" he asked, keeping his voice low. "You didn't make him angry, did you?" He kept his tone accusatorial because he didn't want the young women to feel too confident in their social position aboard the *Corsair*. It was always best, David believed, to keep underlings just a little uneasy, unsure of themselves.

"It wasn't our fault," the redhead with freckles said quickly.

David shot her a chilly look, and she immediately stopped speaking.

The other young woman, the one with jet black hair and the look of a Middle Eastern princess, said softly, "We hardly got started, and then he finished. I thought he'd like a show, so she and I started doing some kissing and touching, and the next thing I knew he's in a barrel going over the Niagara Falls, and he's not coming back."

"You've done nothing wrong," David said, looking into the woman's dark eyes, and thinking that he and Amira really might find her quite entertaining, especially if they used the velvet ropes on her wrists and ankles. "Have a drink. Enjoy the food. Everything is fine."

He could see the heartfelt relief in their expressions, and he made a point of reminding himself that he shouldn't wait too long before he and Amira shared them.

"What's down there?" Tatiana asked David as they sat side by side in chairs on the deck.

"It's an . . . um . . . an entertainment room," David answered after several seconds of uncomfortable silence.

"Like a video room? A gaming room to play video games?"

She has sex with her own sister. She can't be that fucking naïve.

"Something like that."

He was lying, but only a little. There was video in the Dungeon, but the videos that were shown were all XXX-rated. People who blushed easily didn't go to the Dungeon.

"Will you show it to me?" Tatiana turned in her chair, and with the clearest and most innocent blue eyes David had ever seen, added in a soft voice, "Please? I like games."

Fuck. Either she really is the world's greatest actress, or she's as naïve as she seems.

David realized that he wanted to feel Tatiana's slender, young body beneath him as he fucked the hell out of her. In the past hour, while she sipped champagne and sat beside him in the sheer bikini that covered her breasts and hardly covered her succulent ass, David had decided that he would give a fortune if only he could fuck her.

When he realized that this awareness had come to him, he searched inside himself for the voice of reason. After all, when it came to sex, he wasn't a desperate man.

Fuck her at least once. And she's got to give good blow jobs.

With those thoughts dancing around in his consciousness, David was a lot more confident in the way his time with Tatiana was going. He didn't like questioning whether or not he had more social power than the person he was with. Especially not when the other person was a mere slip of a woman, an eighteen-year-old girl who lived with secrets that David could hardly imagine — and wouldn't have, had he not seen for himself the video of Tatiana with her sister, and that ex-boyfriend who had been slimy enough to put the video out onto the dark web.

"Well, will you show me the video room?" Tatiana's voice had a slight edge to it.

David looked at her, sitting there in the navy-blue bikini that hid very little and showed very much, and he realized that it had been a long, long time since he'd lusted after anyone as much as he lusted after Tatiana at that very moment.

"Yes, I'll show you the room," David said after a moment. "But not right now. And I've got to get your sister's permission first."

He watched as Tatiana pouted, and the urge to kiss her mouth hit him with an almost physical force.

"I don't need her permission for anything," Tatiana said softly, so low that even though Svetlana was sitting very close, she couldn't possibly hear. "I'm old enough to make my own decisions."

"Yes, of course you are," David said, also keeping his voice low, thinking that he could very well die if he didn't fuck Tatiana in the very near future. He reached out and patted the back of her hand. "But we don't need to talk about that now. Would you like some more champagne?"

CHAPTER EIGHT

"How did you like your steak and lobster?" Amira asked.
"It was exquisite," Svetlana replied, dabbing the corner of her mouth with a cloth napkin. "Though I feel like I've over indulged. Tomorrow I'm going to have to be very strict with my diet."

Amira's brow furrowed. "You mustn't be so harsh on yourself. You have a lovely body. You certainly don't have to lose any weight."

The sun would set soon, and many of the guests had been flown back to the mainland. Amira had discovered, to her great surprise, that though Tatiana had youth and innocence going for her, her older sister, Svetlana, had sophistication and charm playing in her favor, and that seemed to appeal to her more. At least for now.

Both sisters aroused Amira's libido, and she wanted to have sex with both of them individually, then together, but for the past hour, all she could think about was whether or not the closure of Svetlana's bra was between the cups — and therefore easily accessible — or in the back, which would require a bit more effort, but most certainly wouldn't be an insurmountable task.

And, of course, there was also that little certain something called the most kissable mouth the world had ever seen, which was playing holy havoc with every nerve ending in Amira's body.

"The sun will be setting soon," Amira said. "Let's get some drinks and then go out onto the deck and watch it."

Svetlana looked away. Amira waited, hardly breathing, for Svetlana to speak. She was shocked at how anxious she was for the next words from Svetlana's lips.

"But there are so many people out there." Svetlana looked into her eyes briefly, then looked away. "I . . . I don't feel like being a part of a crowd right now."

"Neither do I," Amira said. She reached across the table and placed her hand over Svetlana's. "I know just where we have to go to watch the sunset and have privacy at the same time." She smiled at Svetlana, and decided to try to set the emotional bondage in a woman she truly didn't know that well. "It'll be just you and me, and we'll be away from these parasites my husband and I call guests. Wouldn't you like that?"

Amira's heart skipped a beat when Svetlana looked her directly in the eyes, and said softly, with her Russian accent adding significant levels to Amira's arousal, "Yes. I think I'd like to be alone with you very much."

Amira rose from her chair and walked over to the bartender standing in crisply tailored livery. She looked at him and smiled benevolently, but when she spoke, there was ice in each word she said.

"I want a bottle of champagne." She inhaled deeply, then exhaled slowly in an effort to control a heartrate that was suddenly throbbing much more quickly than she had thought it would. She gave the bartender the brand of champagne she wanted, and the year. It wasn't the champagne she poured for the businessmen and young women who were partying on the deck one floor above her. They got something less. For Svetlana, Amira had decided that there should be nothing but the best, her own private supply.

"We'll be on the balcony," Amira told the crewman behind the bar. "Serve it immediately, and then leave us. We're not to be disturbed under any circumstances."

"Yes, ma'am," the man replied.

She walked across the room to Svetlana and said, "Come with me. I want to show you the most beautiful place on this yacht, and together we'll enjoy a lovely sunset."

Amira felt her pussy tighten and become more sensitive, when Svetlana looked her directly in the eyes, waited several seconds, then said, "I think I'd like that very much." She closed her eyes and turned her face away for a moment. "I do so love beauty."

Amira waited until they were on the second-floor balcony and the champagne had arrived before she stepped very close to Svetlana. Her own nipples were tight, beaded, and she could see that Svetlana's were also.

A good sign. A very good sign.

The sight of Svetlana's erect nipples made Amira's mouth water.

"To us," she said, raising her champagne glass to clink it against Svetlana's. When they did, Amira was looking into Svetlana's eyes as she took a sip of the champagne, which she had never shared with guests on the yacht.

"My God, that's delicious," Svetlana said after taking a sip.

Amira told her the brand name, and the year, and she was pleased enormously that Svetlana was aware of both the brand, and even more esoterically, the year. There weren't a lot of women who had an understanding of just which years provided the best vintage in champagne.

"I'm glad you approve," Amira said, leaning back against the balcony railing that, not long earlier, she had leaned back against while looking at Svetlana's younger sister. "It's not often I get to enjoy truly fine champagne with a woman who understands such things."

"And it's not often that I find myself with a woman who knows how to seduce. And you do know how."

Amira watched as Svetlana's lips parted, and her breathing accelerated.

"And you have, you know? You haven't kissed me. You haven't even touched me. But I already know that there's nothing you can ask of me that I won't give. There's nothing you can want from me that I won't gladly do." Svetlana closed her eyes, then breathed deeply several times.

During those few seconds, Amira had to suppress the urge to throw herself at Svetlana and simply hope for the best.

"If you don't kiss me in the next few seconds," Svetlana said, "there's no telling what I'm capable of doing."

Amira tossed her champagne glass aside. She heard it hit the deck and break. Later, after she'd had her entertainment with Svetlana, she'd tell one of the servants about the glass, and explain that they had to make sure that there was no broken glass anywhere, since she was often barefooted on this balcony.

But those were issues that could be addressed later. Right now, there was a tall woman standing in high-heels who was nothing less than the very embodiment of everything that Amira found sexually exciting in a woman—and she was there for the taking.

Amira was not much over five feet tall. As she reached up to wrap her arms around Svetlana's neck, she felt both small and wickedly, wildly sexual. Svetlana was the Simonov that she truly lusted for, not Tatiana, who she had thought was her first choice.

Their mouths met, and when Amira parted her lips, she shivered with passion as Svetlana's tongue slipped into her mouth and began to explore.

Amira closed her eyes, and as she kissed Svetlana's mouth and danced her tongue against hers, she wondered whether she would lick Svetlana's pussy first, or if they'd get in the 69 position and do each other simultaneously.

Amira didn't really have a preference, just so long as she wasn't interrupted, because she was in absolutely no hurry to have this tryst with Svetlana end any time soon.

"You're going to kiss me, aren't you?"

The softness of Tatiana's voice and the look of wonder in her blue eyes made the baser instincts in David's soul want to throw her onto the floor. All she was wearing was the bikini, and that was almost like wearing nothing at all. He thought of ripping the bikini off her.

The practical side of him said that it would be more expedient, and certainly more practical and less violent, if he simply untied the knots on the bikini that held it in place, and then he would have complete access to a slender, young body that had been playing on his consciousness since the first moment he'd seen her in the nightclub and had bewitched him from the instant he'd seen her in the bikini.

He'd had sex with more young women than he could remember, but none had gripped his rampant lust as completely as Tatiana. She was, as his wife had said, the ultimate erotic combination of youthful innocence and taboo experience.

She fucks her own sister.

It was a jarring, erotic awareness that David had as he looked down at Tatiana, standing there in the yacht's ballroom, an empty glass in hand, her blue eyes large and round and too sincere for David to think that maybe — just maybe — he shouldn't fuck the hell out of her.

Chances like this doesn't happen many times in a man's life. Fuck her first, then fuck her sister later. So what if I feel guilty afterward?

"Yes," David heard himself say, "I'm going to kiss you."

And then I'm going to fuck you on the floor.

He understood that he could no more stop himself now than he could stop a runaway freight train with his bare hands. Tatiana had ignited in him a wanton, savage hunger that could only be quenched by thrusting himself deep inside her body again and again, not stopping until he poured his cum inside her.

He took Tatiana by the upper arms and pulled her against his body. When he felt her small luscious breasts pressing against his lower chest, a low groan of desire came from his soul. His erection had been twitching and at the ready for action for some time now. David knew that it would only be a matter of seconds before he was at full stature and ready for combat.

When David wrapped his arms around Tatiana's body, it made him aware of just how slender, how small, she truly was. She was a pale-skinned blonde version of his wife. This awareness added fuel to the lusty fire.

He slanted his mouth over Tatiana's, and with almost no hesitation, he thrust his tongue between her lips and into her mouth. He felt her capitulation, her surrender to his dominance after hardly more than a couple seconds, and when he did, his cock went from a living organ to a piece of steel that had masculine desire pulsing through it.

While keeping his left arm around Tatiana, he pushed his right hand between their bodies, sliding his palm over her breast, touching her through the thin barrier of her bikini. He found her nipple and pinched it firmly between his thumb and forefinger. He pinched hard enough to make her squirm and cause a sound to come from deep in her throat.

David kissed her for a full minute before he finally leaned back enough to release the contact of his lips from hers. He stood up straight and looked down into her blue eyes, and the smoldering desire that he saw there heightened the inferno that was blazing in his soul.

"You're a passionate one," he said, his voice soft but raspy with marginally controlled desire. He pinched her nipple through her bikini once again, then let his hand trail slowly downward, his fingertips skimming lightly over the skin of her stomach. "I'll bet you've got a thousand rich men all dying to have you in their arms."

Tatiana shook her head vigorously. David watched as her lips moved as though she was speaking, but no words came out. She seemed very young, and to David at that moment, that was very exciting.

David had been infatuated with women his entire life, but he couldn't recall a time when he was this intoxicated with youthful beauty. Tatiana was in a league by herself. There was no equal to her. There were other girls, and then there was her — but those two things weren't even remotely close to being the same thing.

He kissed her again, though not quite as fiercely as he had earlier, but his right hand drifted downward, sliding now over her stomach and lower abdomen, it's intended target obvious.

David pushed his hand down over Tatiana's hip, moving it slightly to the side to judge her reaction to his more intimate caress. When she made no effort to avoid the caress, David's passion took on a new fire.

He slid his hand between her slightly spread thighs, then pressed his palm against the apex of her legs. He could feel her warmth through the thin nylon.

The first touch is always the best. That's when I know what she's really feeling.

He had always believed that the first reaction was always the most honest, and as he moved his hand slightly forward and backward, caressing the girl intimately but through her bikini, David felt himself to be almost transported back in time to when he himself was a teenager and discovering the passion and pleasure of female companionship for the first time.

David thought briefly of pushing Tatiana down onto her knees so that he could make her pleasure him, but hardly had this thought entered his mind than he dismissed it. His lust was galloping too fast, his wanton desires burning far too hot, for him to be satisfied with just her oral sex. No, that wouldn't be enough. He needed much more than that. He needed to have Tatiana's slender body beneath his own, to feel himself driving into her, burying himself to the hilt into her tender young body again and again until his desire was at last fulfilled and his furious lust was satisfied in the extreme.

Amira's going to be pissed as hell. She wanted Tatiana first.

This awareness didn't stop David from taking Tatiana by the hand, then getting down on one knee and pulling her with him. The thought didn't even slow him down. When they were down on their knees together, he pulled her once more into his arms and sealed his mouth over hers, and as he did, he caressed the cheeks of her ass with both hands, groping her through the gossamer-thin bikini, squeezing tightly, but then reaching around her hip to once again slide his hand between her thighs to intimately touch her.

David allowed her to turn her face aside to end the kiss. He bared his teeth and bit her throat hard enough for her to squeal out in pain. Her high-pitched cry heightened his passion, and he promised himself that he would leave a mark on her body — he wasn't quite certain yet where — before this sexual encounter had reached its climactic conclusion. But one way or another, he intended to leave a mark on her so that she'd remember what she'd done with him — and know with certainty that he could do it to her again whenever he wanted to.

"You're a beast," Tatiana said, but then in sharp counterpoint, she wrapped her arms around his neck and kissed him with a furious abandon that took his breath away. She had that ability, and it shook him to the core.

David untied the bikini string at Tatiana's left hip, and didn't bother with the one on the right side because he now had unhindered access to her pussy, and that was all he really wanted anyway. Only seconds after unknotting the bottom half of her bikini, David was on top of her and between her thighs, his own khaki shorts pushed down, and his fiercely aroused erection throbbing in his hand.

When David thrust into her — very fiercely, and almost full-length on the very first plunge — she let out a short, high-pitched scream, her mouth opening wide, her eyes blazing with a combination of pain and fear.

"Sorry," David said as he withdrew from her velvety embrace, paused a moment, then eased his cock slowly back into her body. He wasn't necessarily a cruel man, just a lustful one, but that sometimes made him dreadful.

She's tight. She's really fucking tight.

David was pleased that Tatiana seemed to adjust to him being inside her after he'd stroked into her several times. He took it as a sign of his size that she had at first felt pain with his penetration. He kissed her neck and earlobe, and promised himself that this wouldn't be the last time that he fucked her. Pleasure this good simply couldn't be a one-off. Besides, he needed Amira to have sex with her, and afterward, he and she would compare notes and, over late evening cocktails, they could decide whether or not she was worth fucking again. David already knew how he was going to vote regarding continued sex with Tatiana.

"Careful," Tatiana said, stroking David's hair as she spoke. "You're big, but I'm not."

That was exactly what David wanted to be told. It did his ego a world of good. He kissed her furiously then and began doing his level best to pound her right through the floor.

He came after less than three minutes. He told himself that she was just too tight to last any longer.

CHAPTER NINE

"This is paradise," Svetlana said quietly, settling back in a chair on the balcony beside Amira. "I can understand why you and your husband spend so much time on this boat."

"The advantage of having a boat is that we can go far enough from shore that we're in international waters." Amira gave Svetlana a teasing smile. "Once you're in international waters, you can pretty much do whatever you want to, and there's no legal authority to tell you that you can't."

Svetlana smiled and raised her champagne glass. "Let's hear it for being able to do whatever the hell we want."

Together they drank, and as they did, Svetlana looked at Amira over the rim of her glass.

If I have to have sex with her, it won't be the worst thing I've ever had to do while on assignment for Omegas Force.

Svetlana realized instantly that she was searching for justification for behavior that she wanted to do irrespective of her mission, and she smiled softly at her own mild self-deception. Under the circumstances, it seemed harmless enough.

"What's so amusing?" Amira asked.

Svetlana shook her head. "Nothing, really. Just an old thought that somehow came back into my head for reasons that I can't think of." She made a dismissive motion with her hand. "It's an old story that's not really worth telling."

"I don't think you're telling me the truth," Amira said, an amused light in her chocolaty eyes, "so I'm going to ply you with more of this delicious champagne, and when I think you've had slightly more than enough, I'll pump you for the truth."

"Then I should probably stop drinking now."

"You could try," Amira replied, her voice very soft, and distinctly sensual. "But I can be very persuasive and determined when I want something."

"And you want me?"

The words were out of Svetlana's mouth before she gave them serious consideration. But once they had been spoken, they couldn't be *un*spoken. She looked directly into Amira's eyes, and for several seconds, neither of them said a word.

"I probably shouldn't have said that," Svetlana finally said.

"Sometimes the things that most need to be said are the words we later tell ourselves we shouldn't say," Amira replied. "Sometimes the most honest truths are the ones that just sort of slip out without us really thinking about them until they've been spoken."

Svetlana finished her drink, then set her glass down on the floor of the yacht beside her chair. She looked Amira directly in the eyes and asked, "Is it safe for me to assume that you and your husband have some kind of understanding? Because if you don't have an understanding, then you and I are just going to have to keep the next two hours our own little secret—because I'm pretty certain my self-control is fading fast."

"My husband and I have an understanding," Amira replied after several seconds of complete silence. "But it's . . . complicated."

Svetlana knew that Amira was lying, at least by omission, but she didn't care.

"Are your nipples very sensitive?" Svetlana asked, her tone hardly more than a whisper. "Mine are. I'm hoping that yours are, too. You see, I've been fantasizing about what pleasure would be mine while I sucked on your nipples, and the more I've thought about it, the more I've been wanting to do it."

Svetlana cupped her own breasts from the underside, lifting the mounds and squeezing them from the outsides to make her nipples even more prominent through the layers of her brassiere and cotton dress. "Look at how hard you've made my nipples, and you've done it just by being so beautiful. See how I respond to you?" Svetlana looked away. "I can't believe I just admitted that. Sometimes I say things that I shouldn't."

Amira rose slowly from her chair, and when she did, Svetlana had to stifle a soft gasp that caught in her throat. She looked at Amira's small, lovely breasts, seeing the aroused nipples that made their presence known through a brassiere and blouse, and Svetlana wondered if her areolas were the color of delicious milk chocolate, like her eyes. She hoped they were. For several seconds Amira simply stood unmoving by her chair, and it allowed Svetlana the opportunity to study her, to appreciate her exotic Middle Eastern beauty as a connoisseur would.

No matter how critically she looked at Amira, she couldn't see her as anything but beautiful.

On a whim, Svetlana asked, "Do you ever go commando?"

Amira shook her head, sending her raven black hair swirling around her shoulders.

"If I asked you to, would you go without panties in public for me?"

This time Amira nodded. A moment later, the pink tip of her tongue moistened her lips. It was an astonishingly erotic thing to see.

"It would be so exciting to know that you weren't wearing panties, and that I was the only person who knew that." Svetlana felt her pulse throbbing in her vagina. "I'd be the only person who would know. Just me. Not even your husband would know." She watched as Amira's breathing became deeper and faster. Now even her nipples were noticeably more erect. "And with every step you took, you would remember that the only reason you weren't wearing panties was because I didn't want you wearing them . . . and I didn't want them because they might get in my way, and you wouldn't know for certain when I would want to raise your dress, get down on my knees, and taste you."

"Oh," Amira said softly.

"Taste you and taste you and taste you for a very long time." Svetlana squeezed her breasts once again, and felt fresh nectar moisten the lips of her pussy. "I wouldn't be satisfied with myself if you didn't come on my mouth at least three times."

"Three times?" Amira said the words as though they contained both magic and paradise.

"At least three times." Svetlana slid just a little lower in the deck chair. "And that would be just the beginning." She began raising the hem of her dress slowly up her naked thighs. "A very good beginning, to be sure, but there would be such good things that would follow." She exposed her panties, wondering whether there was a visible wet spot on the fabric. "So, my darling, I'm thinking that you should probably get down on your knees, take off my panties, and then do what it is I'm sure you do so very well."

Svetlana watched as Amira's gaze went from her panties up to her eyes, down to her panties again, then back up to her eyes.

"Will you kiss me?" Amira asked.

Amira's tone was almost a plea for sympathy, and Svetlana was at that moment in an entirely sympathetic mood.

"For how long?"

"As long as you let me." Amira's voice was barely a whisper.

"Minutes, or hours?"

Amira hesitated, then said, "Minutes. Just a few minutes. That's all." She cleared her throat. 'I don't want you to think

I'm greedy."

Svetlana shook her head slowly, and saw the agony in Amira's eyes. She waited, drawing out the suspense, then said, "A few minutes of kissing simply won't do. A few hours, but not just a few minutes." She raised her dress a little higher. "Now are you going to take my panties off, or do I have to do that myself?"

Tatiana grabbed the sofa's padded arm and held on tightly. She had to—otherwise she would have been driven into the sofa, because David was behind her, and every time he thrust his hips forward, he struck her so hard that the breath was expelled from her lungs, and she was driven forward.

He's fifty and he can still fuck like this? What the hell must he had been like when he was in his twenties?

It was an interesting thought for Tatiana to have, especially since she had already climaxed twice in the past hour. The first time was while she was on her back on the floor with David above her. The second time was while she was on her hands and knees getting it put to her doggie-style while David spanked her.

She had thought that he'd be done after he came inside her, but David had hardly climaxed when he let her know that he wasn't nearly satisfied for the evening. He wanted more of her, and he let Tatiana know that he damned sure was going to get it.

"Not much more," Tatiana said, getting as better grip on the sofa. The sound of a torso striking the cheeks of her ass ricocheted off the walls of the yacht's stateroom. "God . . . you're going to fuck me to death."

There was a certain amount of censure in her tone, but there was also a measure of awe. Tatiana was working on her third climax, which was showing early promises of being even more powerful than the first two.

"Hold back," Tatiana said suddenly. "I'm ... almost ... there."

Three more strokes of a long, hard cock between the lips of her pussy, and climax number three arrived with all the subtlety of a heart attack. Tatiana clenched her teeth and clutched onto the sofa as her insides tightened convulsively, wave after wave of raw emotion coursing through her system while behind her, David churned his hips with demonic fury.

She heard him say a single, obscene word, then groan loudly. She knew that he, too, had reached the pinnacle of passion.

"Yesss," she whispered when she felt David's chest come down to press against her naked back. "Oh, yesss."

If I come again, I could die.

Hardly had this thought gone through Svetlana's consciousness than she realized that it was utter foolishness. She simply would not die if she climaxed again. Logic and reason dictated otherwise, even if her passion said words to the contrary.

But, oh Lordy, the things that Amira was making her feel certainly were good enough to die for.

"If you stop, I'll kill you," Svetlana said.

It occurred to Svetlana that such a threat probably wasn't the proper way to speak to a woman who was sucking rather delightfully on her clit, and pushing her relentlessly toward yet another climax. But once the words were out of her mouth, there was no taking them back, now was there?

Svetlana decided she'd just have to apologize later.

Svetlana closed her eyes briefly, then opened them again. When she closed her eyes, she could more completely concentrate on the feelings going through her, but when opened them, she saw one of the world's truly beautiful women pressing her mouthy intimately against her pussy. Amira's eyes were closed, and her body posture and expression suggested that she was quite pleased with what she was doing.

She's so beautiful.

Svetlana looked through the valley of her naked breasts at the Lebanese woman who was, at that very moment, moving her tongue in a side-to-side motion on her clit, while at the same time sucking on it. Svetlana was impressed — and gratified.

Svetlana said an obscene word. Then she said a string of obscene words. And then she climaxed once again.

It wasn't the garden variety climax that women have. It wasn't just a *well, that felt really good* kind of experience. Rather, it was a *my fucking world is exploding* kind of sensation. It was an *I might die from this* experience.

The one thing that Svetlana was absolutely certain of was that whatever the hell had just happened had to happen to her again. And soon. And often. Because it had rocked her world. To the foundation.

"Stop." Svetlana shouted the word, and with both hands on Amira's forehead, shoved her away. Now post-orgasmic, she was *way* too sensitive to allow Amira to give her any more pleasuring.

At least not until she recovered her breath, regained control of her senses, and could think again in a manner that was both proper and logical.

"Un-fucking-believable," Svetlana said quietly as Amira softly kissed, then nibbled, on the inside of her right thigh. "I thought I was going to die there for a moment."

Amira rather theatrically kissed Svetlana on the inner thigh, very close to her sex. "You know you're delicious, right? I mean, you know that, don't you?"

Svetlana looked at Amira. She was not altogether certain what kind of response she should give. Her time with Amira had produced more climaxes than she had dared to hope for.

Svetlana combed her fingers through Amira's hair. She

watched as Amira kissed her inner thigh again.

"I'm feeling as though I've been quite selfish," Svetlana said, twirling a lock of Amira's ebony hair around her forefinger. "I think that I should make amends."

"You're wrong. There's nothing you have to do. Besides, you made me come four times, and I've only given you three. Lay back and enjoy yourself. You . . . owe me nothing."

"But still . . ."

Svetlana's words trailed off into silence when Amira's tongue once again began working its magic.

CHAPTER TEN

I'*ll never tell David anything. What I did with Svetlana is none of my husband's goddamned business.*

This thought came to Amira while she was sipping her first cup of coffee of the day and thinking about how erotic it had been to be with Svetlana the previous day.

She'd had hopes that their time together would be entertaining, but she never dreamed that the time she shared with Svetlana would be multi-orgasmic.

In the extreme.

Amira had eaten pussy before. She'd had other women go down on her, and she had gone down on other women. Quid pro quo. A woman was supposed to give as good as she got. That was the unspoken agreement.

But with Svetlana it didn't work that way. With her, it was three or four orgasms before she even started to back off. And that was just the beginning. Svetlana caused one climax, and then she caused the second one . . . and after that, the orgasms seemed to pile one on top of the next, some more powerful than others, while others were not quite so bone-shaking, yet still were enormously satisfying.

I'll have to eat her pussy for a year straight just to try to even the score. I've got some serious Karma to pay for.

The thought caused a faint smile to curl Amira's lips. It wouldn't be the worst debt she'd ever have to pay.

If I've got to owe someone one hell of a lot of oral sex, better it is Svetlana than anyone else.

David looked down at Tatiana, sleeping beneath his suit coat on the sofa, and at that moment thought himself to be the luckiest man alive.

He'd spent much of the previous evening making love with Tatiana, and when he saw her first thing this morning, they again had sex. Now she was sleeping, and David was rethinking whether he should give Tatiana away to some politicians just to make money.

He thought about his wife, Amira, but not for long. She was supposed to have been an integral part of the seduction of Tatiana, but she hadn't been. In point of fact, she hadn't known a damn thing about what had transpired between himself and Tatiana.

So much the better.

David pushed thoughts of his wife out of his mind. There was a time and place to think about her, but this was neither the time, nor the place, to give himself over to matrimonial flights of fancy or thoughts of guilt. In fact, quite the opposite was true. What David had to do — what he *needed* to do — was concentrate on the immediate future. And that meant that he would remember that his wife came in second only to business, and that to allow anything to come in his way or might affect his decisions had to be either neutralized or destroyed.

There could be no other way. Business always came first.

But however much David had enjoyed his time with Tatiana, and however much he wanted to have sex with Tatiana and Svetlana at the same time, he never forgot the fact that nothing was more important than turning a profit. And Senator Conrad and Congressman Todd represented the greatest potential he had ever come across. They stood at the top rungs of the political ladder of power in America — and they were corrupt. They were for sale. He knew it, and they weren't ashamed to admit it. The only real question was the price it would cost to buy their souls.

David stepped closer to Tatiana, and for several seconds he simply watched her as she slept peacefully, her lithe, young body covered with his suit coat. The pleasure, the sexual satisfaction he'd experienced with her, was extraordinary.

Beautiful. So beautiful. I'll have to share her with Amira ... eventually. But for now I want her all to myself.

Careful not to disturb her, David lifted the edge of his jacket several inches. Tatiana's legs were curled as she rested on her side. He looked at the sweet cheeks of her ass, and wondered whether she'd ever gone the Greek way. If she hadn't, then he'd be the first, and that would make his climax so much more powerful when he drove his cock where no man ever had.

For a moment he thought of what it would be like to hear her scream as he took her ass's virginity. He'd have to make sure that he used a lot of lubrication, but he also knew that he wasn't a small man, and that the first time she had to stretch to accommodate a hard cock, it would surely be a painful experience.

He could feel his cock, which had recently been satisfied by the young woman, awakening, once again coming back to life. He was fifty now, and he accepted that he wasn't as virile as he had been when he was in his late twenties ... but Tatiana made him young again, and she lit fires in his lust that weren't easily quenched.

I'll fuck her in the ass when Amira's there to watch me do it. That'll get us both turned on.

David smiled. He decided to let Tatiana get some sleep. She'd need it.

"I'm sure that it doesn't say anything flattering about me, but unless a man is a powerful man, a dominant alpha male, then I simply can't find anything interesting about him." Svetlana looked at Amira and smile a bit sheepishly. "I guess the same goes for my view of women." She let her gaze go from Amira's eyes down to her breasts, only partially hidden with a one-sit-fits-all nylon bikini top. "I suspect that's why you can make me come so many times. You're an alpha female . . . and there's nothing about you that doesn't make me tremble inside."

Amira was just about to respond to Svetlana's comment when the sound of an approaching helicopter drew their attention. Svetlana saw the immediate look of annoyance on Amira's face when she saw the helicopter, and she knew the story behind the expression. For the past thirty-six hours she had been in a virtual non-stop marathon of sexual activity with Amira, and Amira wanted that passion to continue unabated — and the men in the helicopter approaching the yacht were most definitely going to put a wrench in Amira's plan for continued sexual excess.

Svetlana looked at Amira and said, "You promised to introduce me." When Amira nodded, Svetlana said, "A senator and a congressman." She lifted her slender eyebrows briefly. Exaggerating her Russian accent slightly, she added, "That's power. That's real *American* power."

Amira scowled, but Svetlana pretended to not see it.

Svetlana's hastily concocted plan was working out nicely. Better, even, than she had suspected it would when it had first slithered through her mind.

Todd looked out the helicopter's window at the deck of the *Corsair* and felt an instant quickening of his heart. There were two women standing near the yacht's heliport, and they were both in bikinis that didn't leave much to the imagination.

As the helicopter drew nearer to the landing platform and as it descended, Todd recognized that the dark-haired woman was Amira — and as David's wife was therefore off-limits and entirely unfuckable. But the tall voluptuous blonde standing beside her was a new face — and a new body — that he hadn't seen before. And, better still, the closer he got to her, the better she looked.

She's not a teeny bopper like so many of David's girls are, but she's gorgeous. Absolutely fucking gorgeous.

Todd looked over at Conrad, and saw that he, too, was paying careful attention to the two women who constituted their greeting committee. Judging by the way Conrad was looking out the window, he was just as approving of the female entertainment that David and Amira had provided for them.

"We've got until Monday morning," Todd said, raising his voice just enough to be heard above the chop-chop-chop of the helicopter blades. "Do you think that'll be enough time?"

Conrad nodded and said, "Sure. I'm not as young as I used to be." Conrad pointed at the statuesque blonde waiting for them. "Let's do that one together. What do you say?"

Todd nodded. "She's not a kid. She's done it before. She'll be able to take it. Do you want her pussy, or her ass?"

"We'll cut cards for it."

"High card gets her ass?"

Conrad nodded. His smile was lascivious. He really wanted her ass, but he'd take whatever he wanted when the first round of fucking was done.

Now that's a body.

Todd reached out his hand, and when the blonde took it, he squeezed firmly, like an experienced politician would, and looked her directly in the eyes.

"It's a pleasure to meet you," he said after Amira had made the introductions. "I hope we can get to know each other better."

With an unmistakable Russian accent that was tinged with sensuality, she replied. "I think I'd like that very much." She smiled. "Actually, I'm sure I will."

And I think I'd like to shove my cock down your throat very much. "You'll be here for the entire weekend?" He hoped the question sounded innocent, though it most certainly was not.

Svetlana nodded, then tugged a little at the top of her bikini—maybe checking to see that it was covering everything it was supposed to.

David and Amira always have the hottest ladies waiting for me when I get here. This one's spectacular.

He wondered about just how much seduction she would require before letting him take off that barely-there bikini. His travel time had been longer than he would have liked, and he was in a hurry to get in his first fuck of the weekend.

Patience, you old fool. This Svetlana's worth wooing.

He looked at Svetlana's lovely face and wondered if she'd pitch a complete hissy fit if he gave her a facial. The young interns he had sex with in Washington D.C. never liked it, though they had the good sense to never complain about it too loudly. Some of the older women weren't so averse to getting a little porn-style conclusion to a sexual encounter, but Todd suspected that was only because they were running out of options.

"I seem to have misplaced my husband," Amira said, reaching out to take Todd's hand, "but I'm sure he's somewhere close. And there's someone else I want you to meet. Her name's Tatiana, and she's Svetlana's little sister."

Todd felt a charge of excitement go through him. Svetlana had a kid sister? Could she be as attractive as Svetlana? The possibilities caused the breath to catch in Todd's throat. When he stole a glance sideways at Conrad, he knew that the two of them were thinking the same thing.

Sisters? What could be better than fucking two sisters at the same time?

Conrad had fucked pussy California to West Virginia, from Minnesota to Texas, and in every state in between. When it came to getting laid, he was no rookie to the experience.

But he'd never fucked two sisters at the same time.

And he wanted to now. He wanted it as he'd never wanted anything in his life. And he pretty much always got what he wanted. Especially when it came to sexual matters.

I don't want to double-team the Simonovs with Todd. I want them all to myself. I want to be the only cock in the bed.

He'd never been a possessive man when it came to the women he had sex with. They were disposable pleasures that were easily taken and even more easily forgotten. But with Svetlana and Tatiana standing in front of him wearing small bikini swimsuits that were as thin as a sheet of paper, he suddenly found himself ridiculously possessive, and as greedy for sexual satisfaction as he'd ever been in his life.

"And what did you say you do?" Conrad asked Svetlana as they stood near the hot tub at the bow of the *Corsair*.

"I work for the family business. We arrange things so that buys and sellers can get together for their mutual advantage, and everyone can turn a profit." She smiled. "I just try to make everyone happy."

Conrad liked her Russian accent. He also liked the way her large breasts struggled to free themselves from the triangular cups of the bikini. If she moved just a little bit too vigorously, he'd at the very least get a glimpse of her areolas. He wanted to see much more than just that, of course, but he had only been with her thirty minutes, and he was still nursing his first whiskey on the rocks, so even though he had every right and reason to fuck her immediately, he was going to be at least a little bit patient.

At least until the sun sets. Once the sun's down, I'm going to put that blonde bitch on her knees, and make her suck me like there's no tomorrow.

It surprised Conrad a little that he lusted after Svetlana

more than he did her much younger sister, Tatiana. Usually he liked the young ones, but there was something about Svetlana that put fire into his veins and made him constantly concerned that he would spring an erection that he couldn't hide. He hadn't been so affected by a woman's allure in more years than he could count.

It wasn't that he didn't want an erection with Svetlana, he just didn't want one when the dozen or so other guests that David and Amira had invited to the *Corsair* might see it. Even on the yacht, a certain decorum had to be maintained.

"I see," Conrad said. He glanced around quickly to make sure that other people weren't close enough to hear what he was saying. He'd spent pretty much his entire adult life in the public eye, and he knew how open mics and overheard comments could destroy a politician's career. "Perhaps we could discuss that a bit more below deck?"

It shocked Conrad at how much he wanted to take Svetlana to the Dungeon. The thought of putting her in handcuffs and then putting her on her knees was like a narcotic to him. He could envision her on her knees, struggling to deep throat him.

He felt a tightness in his chest when he watched Svetlana shake her head, and all that gorgeous blonde hair flicked back and forth over her shoulders.

She was dangerously erotic.

"I can't," Svetlana said, and her tone of voice told him that she knew he was actually referring to the two of them having sex. "My sister is here, and I've got to keep an eye on her." She gave Conrad a subtle, knowing smile. "She's had a couple drinks, and when she does, her good judgment goes right out the window." She closed her eyes briefly. "She has a very passionate nature. It leads her to trouble."

Conrad looked over at Tatiana, who was standing with Todd. She was just as blonde and beautiful, and though

Conrad wanted very much to fuck her, he was more interested in Svetlana. At least for now. He could change his mind, and that wouldn't bother him.

"Your sister is old enough," he said, wanting more than anything in the world to get Svetlana away from the crowd, off the main deck, and down into the Dungeon, where he could do with her sexually whatever the hell he wanted. "She can make her own decisions. You can't make all her decisions for her." Her was trying to sound reasonable, sensible.

Conrad glanced toward Todd and Tatiana again. The two were talking quietly. Conrad let his gaze roam slowly down the young woman's almost naked body, and he started to reassess his priorities. Did he want to fuck Svetlana more than her kid sister? It was a tantalizing question to ponder.

No. I want them both at the same time.

His libido had answered in a declarative sentence. There was no equivocation. After all, he was a member of the Senate, the most exclusive good-ol'-boys club in the world, and therefore he should have the right to have sex with whoever he wanted to, whenever he wanted to, and whoever the hell didn't like that could go fuck themselves.

Conrad smiled. He hadn't felt this lusty, nor this confident, in a long, long time. Getting elected to the Senate brought with it a lot of benefits, and one of those precious benefits was an almost unlimited series of young interns.

Todd looked at Tatiana and wondered whether she often had sex with a man that she'd just met, or if he'd so thoroughly turned on the charm that she was willing to make an exception in his case. What he was certain of was that she wouldn't say *no* when he invited her down to the Dungeon. She'd already made it clear she was sexually willing, even if she hadn't actually said as much.

"Would you like—" he said, but was then interrupted

when Conrad and Svetlana stepped closer. Only being the professional politician that he was kept him from showing his annoyance at their intrusion into his private time with Tatiana.

"Tatiana, you've probably had more sun that you should," Svetlana said. Conrad noted that she had a glass of champagne in her hand, and that it seemed as though she regularly had a glass of champagne in her hand. "It's time to get out of these swimsuits and into something a bit more decent. You go change, and I'll keep these lovely men company while you're gone."

"You're sure?"

Conrad noticed that Tatiana seemed to immediately get into the role of submissive little sister whenever Svetlana spoke to her.

"I put sunscreen on earlier."

Svetlana then said in a softer voice, "Come closer . . . my darling." She glanced at Conrad and Todd, then back to Tatiana. She reached out and lightly stroked her fingers through Tatiana's hair, and when she did Conrad felt the breath catch in his throat. "Your skin is so far, so perfect, it would be a crime to get a sunburn. You've been given a precious gift. You've got to honor it."

What happened next was shocking in the extreme to Todd. He watched as Svetlana bent down, then pressed her lips to Tatiana's mouth. At first it was just a soft, casual kiss that siblings would give to each other. Then it transformed into something much more than that. Conrad could hardly breathe when he watched Svetlana's moist, pink tongue slide out of her mouth, then lightly caress Tatiana's lips. A moment later, Tatiana's tongue did a slow, erotic dance with Svetlana's. It was leisurely and erotic. He knew this wasn't the first time they'd kissed each other like that. He also knew that they were kissing like that because they had an audience.

Holy fuck. They're sisters, and that's how they kiss?

The kiss went on for at least fifteen seconds. When it finally ended, Conrad's erection was half-formed, his pulse was racing, and his lustful curiosity was operating at red line. He hadn't been aroused by anything like that in years. The force of it was shocking to his system.

He watched as Tatiana walked away. Looking at her ass encased in a sheer tight bikini, he promised himself that he'd be fucking Tatiana within the hour.

He simply wasn't going to wait any longer than that. And he was a man who always got the girl he wanted . . . whether she wanted to, or not.

CHAPTER ELEVEN

"She's lovely, isn't she?" Svetlana said to Todd and Conrad. They were watching Tatiana walking away. The men were looking at her in the same way that a wolf watches a lamb when he's got an empty stomach. "She's the greatest sister anyone could ever have." It was uncomfortable to say those words, but she knew they were what the men wanted to hear.

Why does it always have to be about the men?

"You're close, then?" Todd asked.

I just had my tongue in her mouth, and you ask a question like that? "Yes, we're very close," she replied after several seconds of weighty silence. She looked Todd directly in the eyes. "We always have been. Even when she was very young." She sighed softly. "Much closer than most sisters, I suspect."

She saw the reaction in Todd's eyes at the implication of what she had just said, and Svetlana knew at that moment that she had set a hook in the congressman that he'd never escape from.

It was exactly what she had wanted.

She looked at Conrad and asked, "You think she's pretty, too, don't you?"

"Of course I do," he replied. "What man wouldn't?"

Svetlana watched as he took a rather significant swallow of his whiskey. He wasn't nearly as aloof as he was pretending to be. She was determined to put the hook in him, too.

"Or woman." She nibbled on her lower lips for a moment, and the silence in the air was heavy. "Or sister."

She watched as both politicians reacted to what she had just said. While holding her champagne glass in her right hand, she raised her left hand slowly, and did it in such a way that both men paid attention, watching her every move. With her forefinger, she touched herself beneath her left breast, then slowly trailed the finger upward over her breast, pausing briefly at her nipple, then moved higher still. She slid her fingers through her hair at the temple.

"See anything you find interesting?" Svetlana asked, making sure to keep flirtation and white-hot sensuality in her tone. She finished her glass of champagne. "Sometimes these parties that David and Amira have on this boat can be really boring, but I don't think this is going to be one of those times." Her left hand slithered evocatively across her lower stomach, just above the upper seam of her bikini bottoms.

Both Conrad and Todd watched her hand without breathing.

"Did I tell you that both my sister and I find powerful men very . . . appetizing? Especially American politicians." She purred like a kitten. "That's the best kind."

"How fortunate," Todd said, "because both Conrad and I find Russian women to be the most beautiful women in the world."

Tatiana approached them, and the conversation stopped. When they noticed her, Svetlana heard them both inhale sharply and then hold their breath. Men reacted powerfully when they saw Tatiana. Svetlana wasn't entire certain what she thought about that.

Tatiana had changed from her revealing bikini swimsuit into a pair of denim short shorts that were almost as revealing as the bikini she had worn earlier. The pale pink and laced-trimmed camisole-style tank top above the short shorts established the fact that she wasn't wearing a bra. The leather sandals she wore were strappy and virtually without heels. She looked, Svetlana noted with approval, young and innocent and achingly beautiful to anyone who had eyes.

There isn't a person on the planet who wouldn't want to make love to her.

It wasn't necessarily a comforting thought for Svetlana to have at that moment.

"Well," Svetlana said to the men, "now that she's back and you won't be alone, it's my turn to get ready for the evening."

Tatiana stepped forward, smiling, and Svetlana felt her own body react to the girl's loveliness. Once again, she touched Tatiana's cheek with her fingertips, then slid her fingers into blonde hair that was silky. Svetlana wanted to do so much more, but she knew she shouldn't . . . but doing the right thing was often more than just *difficult* when she was with Tatiana.

"Keep them company while I go change," Svetlana said. She bent down and kissed Tatiana on the lips, and once again made sure that when her tongue danced with Tatiana's, the men could see it. But this time the kiss lasted nearly a minute before Svetlana put an end to it. "And no more champagne. At least not until I get back. You know how you can lose all control."

She placed her left hand on Tatiana's breast, and pinched her nipple lightly.

"You probably should have put on a bra, but you have such lovely breasts, it seems a shame to hide them completely." While still caressing Tatiana's breast in an almost casual manner, Svetlana looked at Conrad and Todd and asked, "She shouldn't hide such loveliness, should she?" She gave Tatiana's breast a firm squeeze.

The men shook their heads vigorously in agreement.

So far, so good.

An hour later, in the *Corsair's* great room, Tatiana had time to assess the situation. She felt a lot more confident now than she had when she'd first been with the senator and congressman and Svetlana had been watching her like a hawk.

"I hope I wasn't away too long." She'd only gone to the bathroom, so she knew she hadn't been.

Tatiana looked at Conrad and Todd, and though neither of them were what any woman would consider unattractive, she looked upon them both with utter contempt. They were traitors, enemies of the United States, and for that she could never forgive either of them.

"Of course not, Tatiana," Conrad said, treacle in his tone. Men like him knew how to use the right tone of voice. Or, at least, they thought they did. "I'd wait here all night for you to come back."

Tatiana sat on the bar stool between Conrad and Todd that she had sat on earlier. This time, however, when she sat down, both men put a hand on her naked thighs, midway between her knee and pelvis. It was the intimacy of men who were confident they had the power to do whatever they wanted with women. Especially young ones. There were other people in the below-deck lounge who could see how they were touching her, but apparently they didn't care. And Tatiana knew they didn't. They saw themselves as being above the law, and legions above social censure.

They'll answer for their crimes soon enough. Be cool . . . and remember Svetlana's plan. Stick to the script she's written.

"Tell me something," Todd said. "How often do you come to David's boat? I haven't seen you here before."

"Maybe you didn't notice me," Tatiana said with as much innocence in her tone as she could infuse. "Sometimes I can get lost in the crowd. I think that's because of my height, or rather, the lack of it."

"I am quite sure that even in the largest crowd, you would draw attention." He looked her directly in the eyes. "It surprises me that you don't know that. If you'd spent more time with me, you would know better."

"You flatter me, but then I'm sure you flatter all the girls," Tatiana replied. She turned away, avoiding the kiss that Todd wanted to put to her lips. She wasn't ready to take that next step, even if it was inevitable.

Tatiana looked at Conrad, who was sitting near her. She looked into his eyes, and when she did, she understood immediately that he was a heartless man concerned only with his own good fortune, and no one else's. She saw evil when she looked into his soulless eyes.

I'll fuck them if I have to . . . but I hope when this mission is over, they're both destroyed.

Tatiana had lost all naïve illusions of what her role was at Omega Force. She now looked with clear, unblinking and all-seeing eyes at the future she had chosen for herself.

She looked at Todd and asked, "Do you want to dance?"

She literally couldn't think of another thing to say to Todd.

"Now remember, they can't get satisfaction," Svetlana said, her voice low as she looked at Tatiana. "We want them aching for us. We want them only able to think of nothing more than how good it will feel to fuck us. But the first time we let them fuck us, we lose fifty percent of our power over them. Men love a new conquest."

"I understand," Tatiana said.

Svetlana looked at Tatiana and thought her the loveliest young woman the world had ever known. It was almost impossible to remember that the girl was a deadly assassin working for Omega Force. But it was her appearance that made her so effective as a secret agent working for the United States on missions that would never become public knowledge. She had every outward appearance of being utterly blameless.

Standing motionless in the *Corsair's* clubroom, Svetlana

closed her eyes and tried to remember that there was a time when she had been something significantly more than just a skilled killer.

Then she pushed the thoughts angrily away.

When Svetlana had changed out of her revealing bikini, she had chosen a minidress that clung to her body like a second skin. The U-shaped neckline wasn't particularly revealing, despite the ostentatious beauty of her breasts, though her long, shapely legs were on full display. The five-and-a-half inch stilettoes made her legs look even longer than they were. And with her pale complexion, the midnight black of the minidress heightened her beauty. When men looked at her, they said things they never said in front of their wives.

"There they are."

Svetlana nodded her head toward Todd and Conrad, who stood near the liquor cart, leaning close to each other as they spoke. Svetlana had no doubt that they were saying things that could not be spoken in polite company.

"We've got an hour to amuse then," Svetlana said out of the corner of her mouth, "then the helicopter comes."

"It's just an hour," Tatiana replied. "I can put up with anyone for an hour."

"I promised my sister I wouldn't have any more champagne," Tatiana said as Conrad refilled her glass. She made sure that there wasn't a shred of sincerity in any word she spoke. "I lose all inhibitions when I drink too much." This time there wasn't be a soul on the planet who would doubt her proclamation.

"But you're not going anywhere tonight. Not driving anywhere. Besides, you're with Todd and myself, so you're in good hands."

"I suspect I'll be in your hands before this night is over," Tatiana said, then smiled shyly. 'Oh, my . . . I shouldn't have said that, should I?" She looked away. "But I will be in your hands, won't I?" She looked him directly in the eyes, and then looked away. Her expression was vaguely guilty.

She was standing with Conrad and Todd on the deck of the yacht near the stern, far away from the chaos happening on the bow, and she had been talking with them for the past couple of minutes. They were trying to get her drunk, and they weren't being all that subtle about their intention. She had thought that men of their stature and experience with sexual matters would show a bit more finesse. She could feel the effects of the alcohol she'd consumed in the backs of her eyes, and she knew that she couldn't have much more before it would seriously take a toll.

"You can say whatever you want," Conrad said, moving a half-step closer to Tatiana. "Your sister's not here. You can say or do whatever you want, but the fact is, it's time you make your own life-decisions, and we all know that."

Here it comes.

"But what I want isn't always what's best for me," Tatiana said quietly. "Sometimes, what I want is the worst thing for me."

"Let me decide that," Conrad said as he eased his hand around the back of Tatiana's neck, beneath her hair, to hold her firmly. He bent to kiss her mouth.

Tatiana let him kiss her on the mouth, and when she felt his tongue try to seek entrance between her lips, she initially resisted, but only for a couple seconds. Then she relented.

He isn't necessarily a bad kisser, but he sure as hell isn't Burke. She thought of that for a moment. *But then again, no one else is. Not like him.*

It was a logical conclusion, she decided. The world could have only one Burke.

She let Conrad kiss her deeply, passionately, for nearly a minute before she turned her face aside. The moment she did, Conrad began kissing her neck.

"God . . ."

The single word drifted in the darkness before dissolving on the night breeze. Tatiana looked at Todd as Conrad kissed her neck. She watched as he reached out to brush his fingertips over her face and hair, and the fire she saw in his eyes was carnal lust tinged with a sadism that frightened her.

These are evil men.

The awareness of their true nature made her shiver.

"You like being touched by me," Conrad said, entirely misreading the cause of her shiver. "You obviously want me to caress you more often."

You . . . are . . . a . . . pig.

"This is going too far," Tatiana said softly. Her hands were at her sides, and she made no move to protect her body when Conrad and Todd began fondling her breasts through the cotton camisole. "This is why my sister worries when I drink champagne."

"Your sister's not here," Conrad said as he pinched Tatiana's nipple a bit too hard.

She flinched. It was impossible not to.

"It's time for you to make your own decisions."

Tatiana let him kiss her again, and when his tongue slipped between her lips, she allowed it to without protest, even though everything in her soul was screaming at the injustice of it.

Conrad put his hands on Tatiana's bottom, rubbing his palm against her through her denim short shorts. When he chuckled, Tatiana heard in his tone the sound of a cruel middle-aged man who had immense power and liked to lord that power over the underlings who could not defend themselves against him. Some men were like that. Tatiana suspected that, sooner or later, she'd discover that a *lot* of powerful men were like that.

When these two take the fall, the world's going to be a much better place.

She looked into Todd's eyes as she felt Conrad's lips against her throat, and whispered in a husky way, "Kiss me. I want your tongue in my mouth."

He kissed her then, mashing his lips against hers with such force that she flinched from the pain it caused. Todd didn't seem to notice, or if he did, he didn't care. He forced his tongue as deeply into Tatiana's mouth as he could, and she did nothing to stop him, though she truly wanted to.

"So *there* you are," Tatiana heard Svetlana say, rather theatrically and too loudly, and from very close. "I knew I'd find you eventually, and that when I did, you'd be doing something you shouldn't."

Tatiana reacted as a younger sister would when caught making out with an unapproved suitor by her older sister.

"It's not like what it looks like," Tatiana said quickly. "Really, it's not."

Tatiana saw the fury in Svetlana's expression, and she knew that it was all just an act. But as an Omega Force special operative, Tatiana knew she shouldn't be surprised at all that Svetlana was a superb actress, especially under situations like this. When Omega Force was looking for a skilled trigger finger, it wasn't looking for Svetlana or Tatiana. Their skills lay elsewhere. They were just as deadly, but their skills were of a more sophisticated variety.

"So, you two obviously like my kid sister," Svetlana said, stepping forward, moving very close to the trio. "What's wrong with me? Am I too old to pique your interest?"

Oh, she's good. She's real good.

"I . . . I wouldn't have kissed them if it weren't for the champagne," Tatiana said with a slight tremor in her tone. She was pleased with how her voice sounded. "You know how I get when I've had champagne." She lowered her lashes briefly. "It's a personal weakness, but I promise to be better." She sighed, getting more into character. "I'm very sorry. Truly I am."

Svetlana gave Tatiana a smile. Tatiana knew at that moment that she and Svetlana were on the same wavelength regarding what they had to do to accomplish their mission for Omega Force, and she felt a surge of confidence go through her. The emotion was so powerful and so deep that it was very nearly sexual in how it affected her. Though she was often unsure of herself, at this moment she had no doubts.

"Look at her nipples," Svetlana said, pointing at Tatiana's breasts. "They're hard, erect. Clearly, my sister liked what you men were doing to her."

She's really damned good. She's saying exactly what they want to hear. They're eating this up with a spoon.

"Tatiana, David and Amira want to talk to us about a business matter, so no matter how much you're enjoying your time with Todd and Conrad, it's going to have to come to an end." She smiled at the politicians. "But only for a little while." She touched both men on the cheek with the tips of her fingers. "And when we come back, you can find out for yourselves whether my sister sucks cock better than I do." Tatiana watched as Svetlana lowered her hand, then gave Todd's groin a firm squeeze through his trousers. "Or maybe it's the other way around." She smiled. "I guess you just have to decide for yourselves."

Tatiana was a little shocked when Svetlana kissed her full on the mouth, and caressed her bottom with one hand, while tantalizing her breasts through her camisole with the other.

She heard Todd and Conrad gasp audibly.

Svetlana is a master at this. Those men haven't a chance against her.

Tatiana's confidence in the mission was soaring.

And she kisses divinely

The last thought had nothing to do with the mission and everything to do with her libido.

She could feel nectar moistening the lips of her pussy. She'd never before met anyone like Svetlana, and she knew with all her heart and soul that she never would again. Svetlana was one of a kind.

"What do you mean they're not on the boat?" He was trying hard to keep his temper in check, especially when he was talking to David, but this was almost impossible. He'd had a hard-on because of Svetlana and Tatiana for hours now, and to suddenly discover that they had taken the helicopter back to their hotel in Los Angeles was unthinkable.

"Something happened—it was a business matter, apparently—and they had to leave," David said, making a gesture with his hands that indicated he simply had no power to change what had already happened. "I've extended them all my hospitality, as I do for all of my guests. They insisted that they had to leave immediately, so I satisfied their wishes. Svetlana was speaking Russian very fast and often quietly. I'm sure that has something to do with it."

"I can't fucking believe that this has happened to me," Todd said. "Shit like this simply doesn't happen to *me.*" He made a growling sound in his throat. "I'm a goddamned congressman. I'm on seven different committees. I don't get fucked with."

Except Todd knew that he had, in fact, been fucked with, and there wasn't one fucking thing that he could do to change the facts. Tatiana and Svetlana were no longer aboard the *Corsair,* and no matter how much he wanted to have sex with both of them—at the same time, preferably—he wasn't going to get laid by either of them. No fucking. No blow job. Not even a hand job. Those two gorgeous sisters who did the most taboo, wicked things *to each other* were no longer one of his entertainment options.

I'm in Congress. This shit just doesn't happen to me.

But the facts told a much different story, and no matter how much Todd wanted to believe otherwise, he was a man of facts, even if they didn't tell him what he wanted to hear.

CHAPTER TWELVE

Russell Senate Office Building, Washington D.C.

*Y*ou're fucking kidding me.
The thought shot through Conrad's brain when, while in one of the most famous government buildings in all the world, he looked across the room and saw Svetlana and Tatiana Simonov, looking chic and sophisticated in their designer dresses. The conference was regarding college and university student loans, and more significantly, for student loan forgiveness, and so Conrad and Todd were both there. To not be in attendance would be politically incorrect, and that was a sin those men would never commit.

But neither man had known the Simonovs would be there, nor could they deduce why.

"If I don't fuck them," Conrad said directly into Todd's ear, so softly that no one else in the room could possibly hear, "there is no justice in this world. If they don't suck me, there is no God in heaven. I'll pass legislation that says that have to fuck me, or they'll go to prison."

"I don't think that's going to be necessary," Todd replied. "But I agree with everything else that you've said."

"What the hell are they doing here?" Conrad asked. "This is by invitation only."

"Obviously, they've gotten an invitation. I suspect, my dear friend, you'll find that Tatiana and Svetlana Simonov get lots of invitations to lots of soirees like this miserable event," Todd said. "But also to ones much more interesting than this one."

"You're probably right."

"They get invited to David and Amira Marx's yacht, and that's one hell of a tough invitation to come by."

"Who the hell are they?" Conrad said. "This is the Russell Senate Building, how in hell did they score an invitation here?" It wasn't like just anyone could get into the building. After 9-11, security was very tight.

"Let's find out," Todd said.

"Yes," Conrad said. "Let's find out . . . and then let's fuck them." He looked Todd in the eyes. "I don't give a shit which one I fuck first, but I'm fucking both of them."

Conrad did not like at all the way his chest felt as he approached Svetlana and Tatiana. He wasn't a man who lacked for female companionship. With his money and power, he always had enough women who were more than willing to barter sex for a better life. He got to pick and choose who shared his bed. It was the women who were desperate, not him. And he liked it that way.

But when he looked at Svetlana and Tatiana standing next to each other, he couldn't be angry. All he could think about was just how erotic it would be to have them together, in the same bed, at the same time.

Startling, vivid mental images of the two of them giving him a blow job came to mind, and when they did, Conrad felt his cock twitch and become awakened to the possibilities of adventure. An adventure more arousing than anything Conrad's libido had ever before conjured.

Conrad was twenty feet away from the women when Svetlana noticed him. She smiled broadly upon seeing him, and Conrad's confidence soared.

She didn't leave the boat because she caught me trying to fuck her kid sister. She left for business reasons, just like David had said.

"So, what brings you here?" Conrad asked, his gaze drinking in the beauty of the sisters. Both wore dresses that were stylish, elegant, whispered of great cost, and were not in the least bit revealing. He was impressed. These were obviously women who knew how to play the game. There was a time to show some skin, and a time to be boardroom appropriate. "And you're both looking lovely."

Svetlana looked at Conrad and asked, "What brings us here? Why you, darling. The two of you." With a nod of her head she included Todd. "Things happened, and we had to leave the *Corsair* rather abruptly. I asked my assistant to do some investigating and he found out that you and Todd would be here, so my sister and I finagled an invitation." She gave him a smile that was lush with sensuality. "I do hope you don't mind seeing Tatiana and me again. After all, the last time I saw you with my sister, you had your tongue in her mouth and your hand on her ass."

Conrad felt his heart seize up in his chest. That was *exactly* the kind of thing he couldn't allow anyone to say — especially not in this senate building. If the press should hear what Svetlana had just said, they'd crucify him in print, and on television. And it would be an ugly fucking political execution, and the savagery would go on long after his corpse had been bled dry.

Some senators moved closer, and Conrad knew that they weren't interested in him. They wanted introductions to Tatiana and Svetlana. Conrad was glad to make the introductions. He had made a lot of money that way over the years.

When guests brought out their phone cameras, Conrad was only too happy to oblige — because the photos would show that he didn't have anything to hide. He never had a photo where he was the only man in the picture with Svetlana and Tatiana. The sisters were just members of the audience.

If asked, he'd say something like, "Yes, yes, I remember them. Sort of. Sisters, weren't they? And they had an accent, didn't they?" And that would be the end of the press's interest in the conference.

When they once again had some semblance of privacy, Conrad looked down at Tatiana, then directly at Svetlana, and said, "You're here for a reason, and I want to know what it is." There was steel in his voice, and Conrad was quite pleased with how he sounded. "And don't try to lie to me. I've got the nose of a bloodhound. I can always smell a liar." He paused a moment, knowing the frightening effect it would have on the women. "Talk. Your time is running out."

Actually, their time wasn't at all running out, but he had no intention of letting them know that.

"Powerful men turn us into nymphomaniacs," Svetlana replied, looking unwaveringly into Conrad's eyes. "If you fuck us in the senate building, we'll all come harder than we ever have before." She moved her right hand just enough to touch the tip of her left breast lightly, fleetingly, through her clothes. "And don't tell us that sex never happens here, because we both know that beautiful, young interns have been giving blow jobs to middle-aged senators in this building since it was built."

For the next hour Conrad and Todd mingled with the guests, talking nonchalantly, pretending they really cared about what was happening in the student loan world, all the while trying to make themselves appear rational, reasonable, and most of all, knowledgeable. The truth was that neither Conrad nor Todd could give a shit about the student loan crisis that was looming in the near future, but that didn't really concern them.

It never had, didn't now, and never would.

"This is the room where John F. Kennedy announced that he would be running for the presidency." Conrad made a passing gesture with his hand at the beautifully polished benches lining the walls, then at the other people in the room. "This is also where Joe McCarthy got his great comeuppance when he was asked whether or not he had any decency."

Tatiana gasped softly, then asked, "Seriously. In this room?"

Conrad nodded. "In this room. Actually, not more than twenty feet from where you're standing right now."

Svetlana touched his forearm, and even though he was wearing a button-down shirt and a suit coat, it seemed as though he could feel the heat of her fingers against him through the layers of clothing.

"Can we . . . somehow . . . be alone with you in this room?"

Conrad looked at Svetlana, and thought then and there that he wouldn't mind at all fucking her in this room. But with dozens of cameras all around, and TV journalists practically underfoot every second, Conrad couldn't put to words what he really wanted to do with the Simonov sisters.

I've seen this room a hundred times in pictures, but I've never been here until now.

Svetlana looked around the room, wondering about all the famous and infamous history that had taken place here.

And here she was now, plotting just exactly how she was going to destroy two traitors who, in their hands, wielded enormous power and prestige.

She looked at Conrad and said, "There's got to be some place in this building where you can fuck me."

She saw his reaction of shock and lust, and it was exactly the one she wanted from him. When she looked at Todd, she saw that he, too, was stunned at her bold declaration.

"Are you interested in a show? Something to get things started?" She let her gaze drift portentously to the right, then settle lovingly on Tatiana. "My sister and I are more than willing to provide you a little voyeuristic entertainment." She took a small sip of the disappointing white wine that was being served, and made a mental not to not taste it again.

"Strong men turn me on. I get wet when I'm near strong men. And the two of you—here in this famous building—are the embodiment of power."

Tatiana stepped forward just a little, and said quietly, "I haven't done a lot . . . but I'll do whatever you want. Either of you. I'll do anything you tell me to." Her Russian accent was thicker now than it had been.

"This isn't the building," Conrad said, then cleared his throat. It was clear that he was fighting to juggle his fear of a scandal with his lust. Tatiana suspected there were times when he was more violent than lustful. "Not far from here is where my senate subcommittee meets. There are guards, of course, but I have access to it twenty-four hours a day. And there's a lock on the door.

"You'd fuck us in Congress?" Svetlana asked.

"Both of us?" There was a breathless quality to Tatiana's tone that Svetlana was quite impressed with.

Both Conrad and Todd nodded, then looked around to see if there were any cameras directed at them. Though the room was very large, there were many people in it, and even more importantly, many cameras.

"We can't leave together," Svetlana said. She almost took another sip of the unpleasant white wine, then stopped herself. She looked at Conrad. With her Russian accent a little more pronounced than earlier, she said, "You promise you'll fuck me in Congress?"

"In a subcommittee room. It's where we meet to hammer out deals without TV cameras on us at every minute."

"That sounds exciting," Svetlana replied. "And you can get us in there?"

"I'm a powerful man." He grinned at her. "In subcommittee, Congress fucks every man, woman, and child in this country." He chuckled malevolently. "I can fuck whoever I want."

I'm sooo going to love cutting this prick down to size.

It took some effort for Svetlana to keep her emotions hidden. She told herself that soon enough Karma would play its fateful hand, but this didn't keep her from grinding her teeth.

"When I saw you aboard the *Corsair*, I thought for a moment that I was looking at an angel."

Tatiana looked at Todd and tried to ignore the fact that, only minutes earlier, he had been trying rather sincerely to stuff his tongue down her throat. Fortunately for her, his tongue wasn't long enough to gag her, though she did find the experience nauseating.

"So this is where you decide what will become law?" she asked, pretending that the politician hadn't pulled her dress up and wasn't squeezing her ass through her thong panties.

"Yes," he said with profound self-importance. "This is where we decide how the world is run."

Tatiana looked around. She was surprised that, given the importance of the decisions that were made in this room, it wasn't more impressive aesthetically. There was a table, made of mahogany or oak—she wasn't certain which—and it was very large. The chairs around the table were of heavy wood matching the table, thickly padded and leather-covered, but they weren't the kind of furniture that a billionaire would put in his office.

In fact, even though this was the conference room for one of the most powerful political bodies in all the world, it appeared to be quite commonplace. It wouldn't look out of order if the people who assembled in it were the executives of a mid-sized firm that specialized in selling furniture or hardware.

Tatiana looked at the Congressional furnishings and tried to tamp down her disappointment. She had thought that her government would be more visually opulent than this. When she looked around the congressional room, there was nothing that suggested billions of dollars got spent here. But she knew it did.

"My sister and I have something special for you," Tatiana said as Todd closed the door, and then locked it. "You're going to like it. It's something magical. It's from Russia, and we're certain you've never experienced anything like this before."

She watched as her words sank into the libidos of Conrad and Todd. They both smiled, and she saw their pale faces become just a little more ruddy. Their lust was racing, and Tatiana was going to make sure that they didn't slow down so much as a fraction.

"We have with us an aphrodisiac," Tatiana said. "It's an old Russian formula, and it works one hundred percent of the time. Your cock gets hard, and it stay that way for hours."

"Sometimes three hours," Svetlana said.

Tatiana could see in their expressions that Todd and Conrad liked what they were hearing.

"Sit down," Tatiana said. "There's a certain way we've got to do this, otherwise the aphrodisiac doesn't work the way it's supposed to."

"And this aphrodisiac . . . it's safe?" Conrad asked.

He's always the frightened one. It's amazing he's got the guts to be a traitor to his country.

"My boyfriend in Moscow, and the one in St. Petersburg, fuck me for hours when I give this to them."

She watched his eyes widen, and she wondered why men couldn't simultaneously use their brains and their balls.

Svetlana said, "Sit in chairs, and we're going to give you a show. And then you've got to do everything we say, and you'll have an experience unlike anything that's ever happened to you."

She's good. She knows exactly what to say to press all the right buttons on them.

Tatiana looked to Svetlana for direction, then watched as Svetlana began unbuttoning her own dress. Tatiana followed suit. In only a matter of seconds, both Tatiana and Svetlana were completely naked. The men in the room approved.

When Conrad reached for Tatiana, she danced out of reach. The smile on her face was flirtatious and completely false.

"You stay in your chair," Tatiana said with mock severity. And then, much more softly and with significantly greater sensuality, she added, "Trust me, you're going to enjoy this. Just let my sister and me play out our little game."

Conrad leaned back in his chair. Tatiana watched as he glanced to the side at Todd, and the two men exchanged a smile. They were alpha men enjoying their power.

Soon enough, you fuckers will get exactly what's coming to you.

The thought brought a smile to her lips.

She looked at Svetlana, gazing at her body with no small degree of envy. Whereas Tatiana was petite and youthful, Svetlana was all ripe curves and ostentatious femininity. She was a woman in full bloom. For a moment, Tatiana wondered why any man would find herself attractive if he had Svetlana to make comparisons with. It was not a pleasant thought.

Don't think that way. Nothing good can come from comparisons like that.

"Here it is," Svetlana said, taking a small, green bottle from her purse. She smiled at Tatiana, then at the men. There was nothing but anticipation in every expression. "You guys are in for a night of your life that you will never—not *ever*—forget. I promise you that."

Tatiana felt an emotion go through her that she couldn't name, causing her to shiver. She was not certain whether the emotion was fear or anticipation. All she knew with any certainty was that what was about to happen would involve her, and that in all likelihood, she had little control over what would happen. She was just along for the ride. Svetlana would make all the decisions.

Trust Svetlana. Whatever is about to happen, she's probably been through this before. She's got your back. She always will.

"Get comfortable," Svetlana said to the men. "Now's the time to get rid of those neckties. My sister and I are going to get you in the right mood, and then we're all going to have some fun."

Tatiana's heart accelerated when Svetlana stepped closer, then snaked her arms around her neck. The warm, erotic sensation of having full breasts pressing against her caused conflicting emotions to go through Tatiana. The sensation pleased her, but still . . .

"Kiss me," Svetlana said. It was a command, not a request, and most certainly not a plea.

Tatiana tilted her head back on her shoulders and said quietly, but loud enough so that the men in the audience could hear, "For you? Anywhere. Anytime." She closed her eyes and waited several seconds, and then said, "Anywhere. Anywhere on my body. Anywhere on the planet."

CHAPTER THIRTEEN

If there was anything more erotic than watching two sisters kiss each other intimately, Todd couldn't imagine what it might be. He had thought himself to be too jaded by an adulthood of sensual and chemical excess to be shocked by anything, but when he watched Svetlana and Tatiana kissing, their tongues visibly going from mouth to mouth, he knew in his heart and soul that he was now going into erotic territory that he hadn't even thought of, much less searched for.

From this night forward, every time I come into this room, I'm going to get a hard-on.

He'd spent hours in the room, mostly discussing matters regarding Congress that he really didn't give a damn about. On some occasions, he was so bored that he found it almost impossible to keep from falling asleep. Most of the time he just let himself daydream of young interns who were naïve enough to believe him when he said that had "something special" that the other girls didn't.

Fuck, they're beautiful. He watched as Svetlana and Tatiana kissed, their naked breasts like visual candy for his eyes. He couldn't think of anything he'd ever seen more erotic. *I could come just watching them kiss.*

And then, quite abruptly, the Simonov sisters stopped kissing. Todd watched, hardly breathing, as Svetlana picked up the green glass bottle from the table. Her movements were quick, and jolted him out of his fantasy in an unpleasant way.

"This stuff is magic," she said as she removed the glass stopper. "It costs a fortune, but it's worth it."

She turned toward Tatiana, then poured a measured portion onto Tatiana's forefinger.

Todd could see that the liquid was thick like honey, and very much the same color. He felt himself being sucked into a dangerous situation, but like a moth to the flame, he realized he had no choice but to continue moving forward. The Simonov sisters were an incitement too strong to resist.

Todd could hardly breath as she watched Svetlana and Tatiana smearing the ointment onto their nipples, being careful to cover the entire areolas with the aphrodisiac. He looked to the side at Todd, and he wasn't in the least bit surprised to see that he was caressing himself through his trousers. His cock, though unimpressive in size, was visibly hard.

Todd looked down and saw that he himself had an erection, and he suspected that he was frighteningly close to having a climax. He stopped touching himself immediately. This was *not* the time to shoot his wad before the game had really gotten started. It wouldn't be the first time he'd fallen victim to premature ejaculation. And now that he was no longer a young man, he didn't have extra bullets.

"Come on, my darling," Svetlana said as she straddled Todd's thighs, ignoring the fact that there was a very hard cock tenting his trousers as she settled her weight down upon him. "Suck on my nipples, then have some vodka. The two work together, and when they do, your cock will be as hard as hickory for hours on end." She raised her left breast slightly. The areola and nipple glistened with the ointment she had taken from the green bottle. "Suck my nipples, and then we will enjoy the best night of your life." She laughed. "Don't worry. I've brought lube. You'll be able to fuck me for hours, and I won't even get sore."

Todd opened his mouth wide to suck on Svetlana's breast,

but hardly had he gotten her flesh into his mouth than he backed away, his expression one of utter disgust.

"I know it tastes bitter, but it's worth the effort," Svetlana said instantly. "Kiss me again. Clean my nipple with your mouth, and then you need some vodka to cleanse your palate." She laughed softly. "It's a small price to pay, my darling, so trust me. David and Amira Marx trusted me, and afterward they said they hadn't made love like that in twenty years."

Todd looked up into Svetlana's eyes as she sat naked on his lap. She knew that he was very close to denying her, his defenses now undoubtedly screaming in his brain. She lifted her breast a little higher, and said softly, "Suck on my nipple just a little bit more. Please? I do so love the feel of your lips on my breast."

Svetlana looked over at Tatiana, who was sitting on Conrad's lap and feeding her ointment-slathered breast to him. Conrad, Svetlana noted contemptuously, sucked on Tatiana's breast gluttonously. It didn't necessarily surprise her, though it most certainly disgusted her. But then, virtually everything about him did.

"Now vodka," Svetlana said to Todd, holding a plastic half-liter bottle in her hand. "A nice big shot of vodka with each nipple. It enhances the aphrodisiac."

She tipped the bottle back so that Todd had to take a very big drink of the alcohol. After he swallowed, she gave him another drink. When she watched him sucking the ointment from her other breast, she started counting off the seconds in her mind.

"Time for you to drink," Tatiana said, putting the bottle to Conrad's mouth and tilting it back so that he had no choice but to drink.

She stroked his hair and kept the bottle to his lips. When he stopped drinking, she took the bottle away and replaced it with her right nipple. Conrad didn't complain.

The aphrodisiac was actually a narcotic that, combined with alcohol, caused unconsciousness within sixty seconds, and lasted for sixty to ninety minutes. Svetlana had discovered that the best part of the drug was that it left the victim in a state of amnesia. The men who consumed it simply couldn't remember what had happened to them during the previous day once they had come under the influence of the drug.

Svetlana looked down and watched at Todd's eyes rolled back white in their sockets and his breathing became shallow and even. When she looked to the side, Tatiana was extracting her nipple from Conrad's mouth. He, too, was unconsciousness.

"We've got sixty minutes to make sure these traitors get everything that they deserve."

Svetlana smiled at Tatiana and said, "I couldn't agree with you more completely."

"Get their clothes off, and then we'll start taking pictures," Svetlana said. "I know we've got time, but I'd like to put a lot of miles between us and here when these two bastards wake up."

They stripped the men of their clothes. This was not easy, since neither man was small, and both were unconscious.

Looking down at a naked and limp Conrad, Svetlana looked at Tatiana and said quietly, and with a smile on her lips, "That sure as hell isn't Burke, now is it?"

Tatiana chuckled softly. "Not even close."

"You know, you owe me for that one. I gave him to you."

Tatiana shook her head. "You didn't give him to me, you just loaned him to me." Tatiana's smile broadened. "Thank you for that, by the way. He's . . ."

"Delicious?"

"Yeah. That and more."

Svetlana wasn't sure how she should respond to that. She

and Tatiana had shared many experiences and Svetlana was undecided how she should feel about them.

"Come on, let's finish the job, and then let's get the hell out of here."

Svetlana and Tatiana took turns with the cell phone, taking pictures that would destroy a hundred political careers. There were selfies as they kissed. Then there were photos taken by Svetlana as Tatiana performed cunnilingus on her. Then the situations were reversed. There were photos of Todd on his back with his eyes closed, with Tatiana's face between his thighs. It look as though she was giving him a deep throat blow job, but in reality his cock was as limp as over-boiled spaghetti noodles. But it didn't look that way, and that was all that Svetlana was concerned about.

"Want to get really nasty?" Svetlana asked Tatiana after they were fifteen minutes into the shoot. "I feel a cruel streak coming on, and these bastards really deserve some nasty shit to happen to them."

Tatiana nodded, the smile on her face youthful and delightful, and Svetlana had to resist the urge to kiss her passionately on the mouth, and caress the naked body that was there so close.

As she almost always did, she tried to pretend that her passion for Tatiana was only mission related. She almost always failed.

With some wrestling about, they put a naked Conrad on his back on the floor, then put Todd on top of him, positioning the men so that they were in a 69 position. It looked like they were giving each other blow jobs.

"Let them try to talk their way out of this one," Svetlana said as she touched the button once again on the telephone, clicking yet another photograph. They had taken nearly a hundred photographs.

Then they positioned Todd on the floor, and Tatiana got

above him, straddling his face. His eyes were closed and her pussy was pressed against his mouth. She smiled up into the camera as Svetlana clicked away.

"They'll never survive this politically," Svetlana said as she clicked yet another photograph.

Some minutes later, they had positioned Todd on the floor, face down, with Conrad on top of him, also face down. Their faces were turned away from the camera, but their identities were clear. Anyone seeing the photo had to assume that Todd was being buggered by Conrad.

"We've got enough," Svetlana said. She glanced at her wristwatch. The ointment was supposed to take sixty seconds to take effect, and last for sixty minutes. It had been forty-five minutes since Todd and Conrad had become unconscious, but Svetlana didn't want to push the clock. "This is why Omega Force was formed. Pussy has destroyed more political careers than pistols. Now let's get dressed and get the hell out of here," Svetlana said. "When they come to, they'll never remember a thing, and by then, we'll be on a jet."

"Headed for where?" Tatiana asked.

"Who knows? What difference does it make? We'll be far away from here, and we'll send the photos to Burke, and he'll send them to all the right people.

"This cannot reach the light of day." The Speaker of the House looked once more at the digital photograph of one of the most powerful members of Congress, who seemed to be having anal sex with one of the more influential members of the Senate. Both of them were naked. And judging by what he could see of the room they were in, they were doing the *wild thing* in one of the conference subcommittee rooms.

"You'd think they'd have the decency to get a hotel room," the speaker said.

"It gets worse," his aide said. "The women they were with . . . they're Russian."

"Fuck." The Speaker's shoulders slumped.

"And not just Russians of the garden variety type." The aide cleared his throat. He was clearly nervous. "Are you sure you want to hear this right now?"

The Speaker clenched his teeth for a moment, then said in a declarative tone, "You're fucking right I want to hear it now."

"The two women are sisters, and they're probably the illegitimate daughters of one of the founding members of the Russian Mafia. Our government has been hunting him for years . . . without success."

"Fuck." The Speaker closed his eyes. "Those two pricks have just resigned their positions. Politically, they disappear as of right now. None of this ever gets to press. Those pricks disappear and we put new people in their places. Is that clear?"

"Yes, sir. Perfectly clear."

The End

About the Author

Robin Gideon is the author of over 50 novels and novellas in paperback form and for e-publishers. She is currently writing erotic action-adventure stories starring the secret agent Svetlana Simonov exclusively for eXtasy Books. This is her fourth story starring Svetlana Simonov. She can be reached at robin.gideon@ymail.com.

www.ingramcontent.com/pod-product-compliance
Lightning Source LLC
Chambersburg PA
CBHW060629130626
46555CB00002B/726